I0575516

The Screenplay Series

OXYGEN WARS

Oxygen Wars

All Rights Reserved © 1991 by Melton Eduardo Cartes, Daniel Merritt

No part of this book may be reproduced or transmitted in any form or by any means, graphic, electronic or mechanical, including photocopying, recording, typing, or by any information storage retrieval system, without the permission of the publisher.

AlbinoPigGorilla Press

For information:
www.meltoncartes.com
www.albinopiggorilla.com

ISBN: 979-8-9943732-0-0

Printed in the United States of America

This is the screenplay originally written
around 1991 that was then novelized around 2006,
which is available in paperback, e-book, and on Audible.

This screenplay is part of
The Screenplay Series of published screenplays,
in paperback and e-book.

OXYGEN WARS

an original screenplay

written by

Melton Eduardo Cartes

&

Daniel Merritt

FADE IN:

THE DISTANT FUTURE...

EXT. THE DIRT PLANET - DAY

A rust-colored world of sand and rock. Not Earth. Not Mars. Way farther away.

The sky is poisonous yellow in this desolate place. It IS poison.

The silence of the landscape stretches across the planet, sporadically interrupted by irregularities, such as...

A DUST STORM...that approaches, completely obscuring everything. Soon, even the backdrop of distant ridges and badlands is gone.

As dust subsides the broken terrain peeks through anew.

A MASSIVE SILHOUETTE. A rocky butte? A mountain? No. As the disturbance passes, it's clear it's man-made.

A TOWER, like a nuclear plant, looms over the landscape. It features a weather-beaten stylized graphic of a tree; a cynical marketing joke on this planet.

EXT. NEARBY RIDGE

FIGURES huddle together. Scores of them. Facing downwind from the storm.

One of the figures turns to stare at the Tower in the valley below. This is ANGUS 7873. 40ish.

As it says on their armor, these are COLONIAL MILITANTS: haggard, death-warmed-over sealed permanently in armored spacesuits, bristling with weaponry.

Their suits triple their body size.

Their armor is emblazoned with a literal
patchwork of logos, an armor plate soldered
on top of another, the result of salvaging
from dead soldiers, brand equity long
ago lost: GeoConSo, PetroCom, InfraSpace,
ExxoCon.

                    ANGUS
          ...look for the blue sky...

They all turn to the Tower, patient as the
stones around them. But, not inert. The
waiting ATTACKERS.

THE TOWER...

Massive sliding doors slowly part. LIGHTS
blink on in the Tower's dark interior,
headlights, or headlamps. More and more
lights hesitatingly come on.

Angus' attackers shift their weight and
fidget like the nervous horses before the
Charge of the Light Brigade.

                    ANGUS
          Look for the blue sky.

All of the Attackers hear a CHIME in their
helmets.

                    ATTACKERS
                  (in chorus)
          Look for the blue sky!

EXT. COMMAND CENTER

Elsewhere on this barren world sits a
building as big as a battleship.

INT. COMMAND CENTER

COMPUTER SCREENS display a screensaver

logo: BUDDHA. The computerized nerve and command center for Colonial Militants. There are work stations and seats, but NO ONE is here now...

ON Buddha's computer screen: TERRAFORMING PLANT status; Nominal ATTacker/DEFender balance; 100/40. GO MISSION. GO MISSION. GO MISSION.

EXT. PLANETARY ORBIT

A satellite, one of many, designated OS17 flies by, giving Buddha constant contact with the surface; a system of advanced remote control.

EXT. THE RIDGE

The Attackers fan out swiftly.

A BEAM OF LIGHT...SLICES from the open doors and blows the Attacker standing next to Angus to pieces. Angus doesn't flinch as pieces bounce off.

                    ANGUS
                 (filtered mic)
          Tycho Buddha. Defender
          response. Defender response.

More beams of light slice out of the Tower.

CLOSE ON an ANTENNA HUMP, ENET-1, on Angus' "neck."

INT. COMMAND CENTER

Angus' speech types out. Buddha's computer screen holds a moment, changes to: DEFEND MODE!

EXT. THE RIDGE

Angus and the Attackers watch as the figures inside the tower base slowly emerge into the Dirt Planet's daylight.

THE DEFENDERS of this Tower.

They're exactly like Angus' group except that they have different orders. Each soldier bears a close family resemblance to someone on either side of the battle.

Angus waits. Buddha sends back a CODED RESPONSE. The second Angus hears it he shoulders a heavy cannon, takes a deep breath, and...

                    ANGUS
                  (yelling)
         LOOK FOR THE BLUE SKY!!!

All hell breaks loose.

EXT. TOWER BATTLEFIELD

EXPLOSIONS. SHRIEKING GUNFIRE. LASERS slicing through the air. Smoke, sand and debris. Some Defenders fall.

                    ANGUS
         Four Defenders. One dead.

SPELVIN, 30s, an Attacker, pauses amid the clash with Defenders. He looks at Angus.

                    SPELVIN
         Two Attackers down.

Grenades land near Spelvin. Another ATTACKER behind him is blown into fragments. Spelvin doesn't need to see; his suit's data screens inform him.

                    SPELVIN
         Three Attackers terminus.

Angus wheels around and fires at ROACH, a
Defender, but only scores a glancing blow.
Roach angrily turns on him.

                    ROACH
          Miss.

ROACH fires a rocket at Angus.

Angus staggers to the side; the rocket
CLANGS off his armor. Doesn't detonate. It
glances off the ground, kicking up broken
rock before EXPLODING in the air.

ANGUS regains his balance and fires
another burst, TEARING ROACH'S TRANSPARENT
FACEPLATE off his helmet. Roach gasps,
stunned.

                    ROACH
          No! No! Help! Help...!

Roach's lungs fill with atmosphere.
Immediately he drops his weapons and
starts to CONVULSE. His skin sizzles and
breaks into weeping blisters. BLOOD leaks
from his eyes, nose and ears.

Angus stares at him impassively. But a
slight facial tic suggests something more.

Roach falls, screaming in human pain. And
as he dies, he reaches out for the Tower
he'd been defending.

                    ROACH
          Forgive me Tycho Muhammad.
          Help me...

Roach dies staring at the Tower, and slowly
corrodes.

Angus turns and stares at the Tower, built
to gradually replace the deadly atmosphere
with oxygen, to turn the Dirt Planet into
a Green Planet. Like Earth.

                    SPELVIN
          Tycho Buddha. Penetrate
          Tower perimeter.

                    ANGUS
          Excellence. Breach imminent.

                    CALVIN (O.S.)
          Negative. Negative breach
          imminent.

Angus and Spelvin react. A Defender,
CALVIN, 30s, has the jump on them. Battle-
scarred Calvin is mostly GeoConSo.

Calvin unloads a particle beam on Spelvin.
It's a direct hit; Spelvin EXPLODES.

But suddenly Calvin comes under heavy fire
and has to fall back. Angus notices the
name on Calvin's armor.

                    ANGUS
                  (grimacing)
          Calvin...

Angus has a collage of logos, but at one
time he belonged to Petrocom. He turns to
engage another pocket of Defenders trying
to regroup, thoughts back on the battle.

Calvin surveys his followers falling all
around him. He turns and looks at the
Tower.

                    CALVIN
          Tycho Muhammad. Defender
          rank declining. Require
          air support.

Calvin blinks... And then a coded RESPONSE
sounds.

                    CALVIN
          Blessings from Muhammad.

INT. AUTOMATED HANGAR

A dark shape in a dark room. Like a
gigantic insect. Lights flash on in this
warehouse-sized space, illuminating...

THE FLYING VEHICLE...as it comes to life.
Automated fuel couplings disengage and the
entire ceiling yawns open. Red and yellow
lights spin.

SAND. WIND. NOISE. The Flying Vehicle
levitates.

INT. THE FLYING VEHICLE

The battlefield comes into view in front
of the windshield. Two EMPTY SEATS are
silhouetted against it. It's automated.

CLOSE ON A SCREEN: All the Attackers are
outlined as glowing, numbered targets in
an aerial view of the battle.

EXT. TOWER BATTLEFIELD

Angus looks up at the Flying Vehicle.
Suddenly...

Hell rains down from it. Attackers
everywhere are blown to pieces. Angus
scrambles for cover.

INT. COMMAND CENTER

Buddha's screen instantly updates the
carnage the Flying Vehicle is causing:
ATTacker/DEFender balance: 90/27 Defender
rank 30%.

Then: ATTacker/DEFender balance: 72/26
Defender rank 36%.

Then: ATTacker/DEFender balance: 35/26
Defender rank 74%.

EXT. TOWER BATTLEFIELD

A bolt from the Flying Vehicle just misses
Angus. Despite his size, he moves fast. He
stops. The Flying Vehicle roars by, to turn
around and make another pass.

                    ANGUS
          Tycho Buddha. Heavy casualties.
          Withdraw. Withdraw.

He starts to run back towards the ridge
they came from.

But, CALVIN...body checks his armor into
Angus. Angus whirls around to square off
and grapple. While in the sky, the Flying
Vehicle circles back.

INT. THE FLYING VEHICLE

On the Flying Vehicle's screen, Angus'
target and Calvin's indicate: Loyalty
Conflict! Friendly Fire Danger!

The Flying Vehicle considers a moment, then
makes a decision: <u>Override</u>.

EXT. TOWER BATTLEFIELD

The Flying Vehicle's aim adjusts. A BEAM
turns the ground white behind Angus,
sending them both flying, end over end,
into a ravine.

                    ANGUS
          TYCH#@...DDHA. TYCHO*S!BUDKL!

The Enet-1 antenna hump CRACKLES as it
burns out. SPARKS fly from it. Angus flies
through the air as he...

FLASHBACK

Blurry shapes. CRYING, a toddler in an

incubator. A gloved hand, finger reaches
down and wipes away a tear. The toddler
blinks at being touched. The hand
lingers...

END of FLASHBACK

...and smashes into a ravine, a singed
Calvin landing right near him with equal
violence.

Angus' eyes are closed. His armor is
ripped up. Burned.

The battle dies off. Silence.

Colonial Militants, both Attacker and
Defender, litter the entire landscape. Lost
appendages, dropped weapons, spent shells
are everywhere.

The few remaining Defenders walk back
into the Tower, their dead left on the
battlefield.

                              DISSOLVE TO:

EXT. TOWER BATTLEFIELD - TWILIGHT

A shadow jiggles behind a boulder. Slowly,
timidly, a squat shape — only a few inches
high — peeks out.

This is a REPAIR CRAB: A small, service
robot with a cluster of tiny eyes, legs,
claws, and a ridiculously long name (P-Vo/3
1417800014307097412098970123431073243), one of
many "species" of repair crabs.

P-Vo tests the air, like a field mouse
sniffing for predators or something to
do. P-Vo seems to determine it's safe, and
scurries into the open.

P-Vo picks its way over to a fallen
Attacker. CARTER, 40s. A soldering device

deploys from P-Vo and starts to weld one
of Carter's dislodged armor plates, hanging
at an angle, back onto his body. Carter's
leg kicks.

More repair crabs emerge from the suits
and every hidden spot on the entire
battlefield. Thousands of them, all
repairing Colonial Militants.

Now the battlefield shimmers in the
twilight from the activity of the thousands
of repair crabs. It's like a beehive.

One regiment of tough little crabs
specifically focuses on an area of Carter's
damage as they all, in perfect sequence,
hammer a mangled armor plate back into
shape.

Carter's suit's running lights come back
on. His data screens do too and go through
a diagnostic. Images and text play spookily
over his face. Until...

Carter's eyes open. He pushes himself up
and rolls over. Several crabs get stuck
beneath him and then crawl away.

Carter gets to his feet, practices some
quick draws with his various weapons. He
lets out a strange, mechanical yawn and
then speaks.

                    CARTER
          Buddha? Carter reporting
          one hundred percent rehab
          and ready.

A response signal sounds. Carter starts to
wander away.

Crabs pull the dead Defender, Roach, out
of his armor and break up the suit for
spare parts. In a short time these tiny
"creatures" expertly disassemble the armor,

cables and surgical tubing.

The dead man is discarded like a snail out of its shell. Now fully exposed to the corrosive atmosphere, Roach's body starts to smolder and degrade.

Repair crabs similarly swarm over Spelvin's suit. One detaches itself, dragging several pieces, and heads to...

EXT. THE RAVINE BOTTOM - NIGHT

Where it makes a slow but sure bee-line to Angus.

P-Vo is already there, trying to work on the burnt out antenna hump at Angus' neck.

A group of crabs have repaired the antenna hump hardware and leave. The old antenna hump is a hunk of melted alloys lying in the sand.

But P-Vo can't seem to get the new circuit board to work in the repaired antenna hump.

P-Vo goes and picks through the spare parts the new crab brought over. There's a communications board from Spelvin that looks just like Angus'.

The two crabs get in a nasty tug-of-war. P-Vo prevails.

It drags the communications board over and switches them. But as the repair crab's appendages poke, prod, and solder the new communications board...CRACKLES and SPARKS. P-Vo backs away, spooked. And then it stares.

Finally, P-Vo slumps. It seals a panel over the burned-out circuit board and scrambles away to its next job.

EXT. BATTLEGROUND

The Tower stands haughtily. Spotlights
illuminate it as it hums and operates.
Millions of tiny lights swarm the
battlefield. The repair crabs, busily
working under the gaze of twin moons.

                              DISSOLVE TO:

EXT. BATTLEGROUND - DAY

A Colonial Militant stirs, the scarred and
burnt name HAGEN on her armor. The human
being inside, 40s, is a haggard veteran of
many battles. Her arm and a leg stir again
as she lies face down in the sand.

Repair crabs emerge from tunnels they've
dug underneath and crawl all over, going
about their business.

Her suit comes on, goes through the
diagnostic. Her own expressions seem to go
from dead sleep to consciousness as the
diagnosis processes to an end and her...

Eyes open. She pushes herself up to her
feet and does the mechanical YAWN followed
by...

                    HAGEN
          Buddha? Hagen reporting
          one hundred percent rehab
          and ready.

The same response SIGNAL. Hagen gets up
and wanders away with her laser cannon at
port.

Six or seven repair crabs carry a piece of
armor to Spelvin.

The crabs stop, think better of it,
turn and carry the armor to Angus and
immediately weld it on him. Angus stirs.
The diagnostic begins as his suit comes

on.

The diagnostic finishes and Angus opens
his eyes and sits up. Parts of Spelvin's
helmet lie near Angus. He looks at it for
a moment. ANGUS DOES NOT YAWN.

Calvin stirs next to him, going through
the same process, YAWNS...

                    CALVIN
          Buddha? Calvin reporting
          one hundred percent rehab
          and ready.

Calvin gets the acknowledgement and
gets up. Angus looks around. Crabs are
dismantling Spelvin's parts. Angus looks
at his data screens: 99.99973 % rehab and
ready.

                    ANGUS
          Buddha? Angus reporting
          ninety- nine point nine, nine,
          nine, seven, three percent
          rehab and ready.

Waits.

                    ANGUS
          Buddha?! Angus reporting
          ninety- nine point nine, nine,
          nine, seven, three percent
          rehab. Ready. Respond.

Angus gets up. HALF OF THE RESPONSE SIGNAL
COMES THROUGH.

                    ANGUS
          Incomplete.

Angus frowns, looks at his data screens.

                    ANGUS
          Re-send.

Calvin looks at him. The acknowledgement comes through again, but incomplete. Angus hits his helmet. Looks at all the data screens. Nothing. No warning. No malfunction. He types a combination.

One of his data screens show: Repair Mode, COMLINK. Angus' suit does another self diagnosis. His data screen: <u>COMLINK — 100% integrity</u>.

Without a battle, Angus and Calvin are neither Attacker nor Defender, they're "BETWEEN DUTY," as indicated by Calvin's data screens in his helmet. He's oblivious to Angus as he looks around, about to wander off.

                    ANGUS
          Calvin.

                    CALVIN
          Tycho Muhammad. Vector
          seventeen das twenty eight,
          Orlando.

                    ANGUS
          Calvin. Tycho Buddha. Ready.

Calvin stares at Angus without reaction. Angus is trying numerous variations of communication protocols.

                    ANGUS
          Tycho Buddha. Tycho Buddha.
          Ready.

Calvin turns around and walks away. He wanders in the same direction as the others.

                    ANGUS
          Calvin. Calvin. Tycho Buddha.
          Tycho Buddha. Ready. Ready.

Calvin ignores him. Angus gets worked up.

                         ANGUS
              ...wait.

Angus watches as one by one all of the
rehabilitated soldiers disappear over
the horizon. He desperately tries to
communicate with someone, anyone. The more
they ignore him the higher his voice gets.

He seems unused to making the facial
expressions that are occurring on his face.

                         ANGUS
              ...Tycho Buddha stay...Tycho
              Buddha stop... Wait.

Angus watches the last soldier on the
plain become a dot on the horizon and
then...blink out of existence leaving
Angus...

ALONE.

Angus BLINKS, frowning, confused.

Angus seems to go from plain thoughts to
anxiety and back to plain thoughts as he
stands there. Long pauses interrupt these
emotional moments, where he just stares out
of his helmet.

                         ANGUS
              Tycho Buddha. Ready.

He shifts his weight, sighs, blinks. He
glances at the tracks left by the soldiers.
Gradually, ever so slowly, an IDEA occurs
to him.

                         ANGUS
              Tycho reticuli Buddha?

He waits for an answer.

                         ANGUS
              Tycho reticuli Buddha?

The sun drops below the horizon, leaving him in darkness, trying to connect.

He follows them.

EXT. ROLLING HILLS - NIGHT

Angus' helmet lights track the footprints ahead of him.

                    ANGUS
          Tycho system Buddha!

He clears a ridge. Two gorgeous planets fill the sky, striped by dark cirrus clouds.

                    ANGUS
          Tycho system Buddha.

Way up ahead, Calvin hears Angus. But his lack of expression suggests it doesn't mean anything to him...

                    ANGUS (O.S.)
                  (filtered)
          Tycho system Buddha. Respond!

...so he says nothing.

                    ANGUS (O.S.)
                  (filtered)
          Tycho system Buddha. Respond.

No response. Angus sighs.

LATER

A tiny little Angus climbs a big hill diligently.

                    ANGUS
          Tycho barada Buddha. Respond?

EXT. HILLSIDE - SUNRISE

There are dots in the distance. Angus
follows them.

                    ANGUS
          Tycho Buddha barada Buddha.
          Respond?

He waits. And waits. And waits. NOTHING.

His data screens display a lot of
information. One of them is always showing
the time as a digital counter that
constantly rolls numbers.

                    ANGUS
          Tycho Buddha nikto Buddha.
          Respond?

Angus looks at the time and watches the
numbers scrolling. The seconds are a
blur, minutes are slower, hours slower
still; days, weeks, months, and years are
irrelevant.

                    ANGUS
          Seconds. Minutes. Hours.
               (pause)
          Days,...weeks,...months,...

He falters in his steps.

                    ANGUS
          ...years.

EXT. VALLEY - MORNING

Alone.

                    ANGUS
          Tycho Muhammad. Respond.

Calvin's eyes turn. He heard it. Angus is
bored.

                    CALVIN
                   (filtered)
          Orlando forward. Forty two,
          two, eleven. Excellence.

Angus snaps to attention. He's been
acknowledged!

EXT. PLAIN - DAY

Angus catches up to the others. His face
is an almost child-like expectation.

                    ANGUS
          Look for the blue sky.

                    CALVIN
          Designate.

Angus' data screens indicate the names
of all the soldiers standing around him.
There are TEN OF THEM from the repaired
group that left the battlefield.

Calvin's data screens indicate a schematic
of Angus but no identification, no
DESIGNATION — FRIEND OR FOE. It's as if he
doesn't exist.

                    ANGUS
                   (filtered)
          Angus. Seven eight, seven
          three!

A cursor scrolls down directories as Calvin
calls up that number on his screens: No
contact, KIA (Killed In Action).

                    CALVIN
          Angus, seven eight, seven
          three has been Killed in
          Action.

Angus' vital statistics jump as his blood
pressure goes up from his anxiety. Angus

becomes frantic.

                    ANGUS
                  (filtered)
          Negative. Angus seven
          eight, sev...

Angus watches them in confusion, his I.D.
number, 7873, clearly labeled on his armor
along with his name: ANGUS. Calvin turns
to continue walking. BEEEOOOP. An alarm
goes off in all of their suits.

                    CALVIN
          Rest period.

All of the soldiers sit down, except Angus.
THEY IGNORE HIM. He walks around them.

They all have switched to REST MODE, all
at half power. Except for Angus.

Angus studies their faces. Some of their
eyes flutter. He stares at MONICA, 30s, one
of the soldiers. Her lips move silently...
Why?

Her faceplate goes opaque. He looks at
the others and their faceplates have gone
opaque as well.

Then, the same images start playing on all
their faceplates, these are personal movie
screens. Angus is basically watching these
from behind the movie screen.

It's happy images of people running through
fields of grass in a beautiful world with
a blue sky. Angus watches as if he's never
seen this before.

Things Angus doesn't recognize populate
these images, a dog playing with the
people, birds flying in the sky, flowers,
trees, not to mention the grass and the
blue sky.

REST MODE. He doesn't get it. He looks at
the sky; dirty. He looks at his data screen
flashing the words REST MODE and selects
it. His faceplate goes opaque and displays
the same video, already in progress.

Angus is confronted with the images of men
and women and smaller versions (children)
running around and laughing. The LAUGHTER
sounds so strange to him.

The video ends as Angus is rearing back,
assaulted by the images in his helmet.

Finally Angus sits down, tired. Next to
Monica. Monica's suit starts to feed her,
same as the others.

But not Angus' suit. He stares at them.
Looks at his own suit. Thinks. He scrolls
down his data screens.

Suddenly

                    MONICA
          This guy walks into a bar.
          He tells the bartender,
          pissfuckshit. Laughs and
          laughs. I bet him five
          hundred dollars.

Just as suddenly. The soldiers laugh.
Mechanically. Forced. Angus stares at
Monica.

                    CALVIN
          This woman walks into a
          bar. Guy says what are you
          doing with that pig. She
          says, Okay where's that
          bear. The dog.

Angus looks at Calvin. Again the soldiers
laugh, as if programmed to laugh. Eustus,
male, 20s, tells a joke.

                    EUSTUS
          Three whores are talking to
          each other. I'll grant you
          three wishes. Paint my house.

The soldiers laugh. Angus stares at
them, studies his data screens, scrolls
down a menu. There! Data Screen: Food --
FGST 8766584. He selects it and his suit
dispenses nutrients into his bloodstream,
according to the screens.

                    GARTH
          City folk stop at a farm.
          Farmer says they stop to
          talk to him.

Angus looks at GARTH, male, 20s.

                    GARTH
          There's a pig in a pen.
          Why's that pig got three
          wooden legs. You don't eat
          a pig saves the house.

More canned laughter. Angus is lost.

Angus looks at his data screens and
notices a blinking selection: REST MODE/
DIVERSION. He selects it and accesses the
jokes file. Leni, female, 30s, tells a joke.

                    LENI
          Two policemen stop a
          horse. The horse tells
          them to take a hike. Don't
          know what to do with it.
          Makes a million in the
          stock market. Two to turn
          the horse, one to write
          the report.

More pre-programmed laughter. Angus has the
same jokes on file and reads along: Two to
turn the horse, one to write the report.
GotoCode^X2377 ^Laughter^ 86 **.

Angus stares out at them. They laugh and then stop abruptly. A joke appears on Angus' screen: A man picks up his mother-in-law. His wife needs a face lift. Every time she kisses her on the cheek. Happy.

No one says it out loud. It blinks insistently at him unlike the other jokes did. Angus studies the others, wondering. The joke stops blinking on screen and switches to "GotoCode^X2377 ^Laughter^ 86 **."

All of the soldiers laugh mechanically again, startling Angus, laughing at "his" untold joke.

Another one tells a pseudo-joke that has come on screen. Again they laugh. Stop. On and On. Angus looks up at the rusty sky.

                    ANGUS (V.O.)
          ...look for the blue sky.

One thing these soldiers can do is wait for long periods. The sky darkens. Bluer. Stars peek through.

Their pseudo jokes drift into the darkening night sky and FLOAT UP TO SPACE as aimless radio noise.

An orbiting satellite hears the jokes as it watches over the dirt planet and the crescent of day wanes in an expanse of black.

                                        DISSOLVE TO:

INT. LABORATORY - DAY (FLASHBACK)

A teenager is standing, wearing a grey jumpsuit, tubes and wires attached to it. Machines patch wires to his head. Laser scan-lines flash across his face. It's Angus as a teenager.

                    ANGUS (V.O.)
          ...look for the blue sky.

A ROBOTIC ARM swings over him.

                    ROBOTIC ARM
          Look for the blue sky.

Other robotic machinery moves into action
as young Angus is placed on a work table
or bed. Arms move pieces of armor into
place and start building the armored space
suit he'll live in from now on.

                    ANGUS
          Look for the blue sky.

All the heavy machines moving about him
are scaring him. He stares at all of it.
His voice is rising with his anxiety.

                    ANGUS
          Look for the blue sky!

Auto-welders solder sections together.
Probes test motors and systems in the
suit.

                    ANGUS
          Look for the blue sky,
          look for the blue sky,
          look for the blue sky,
          look for the blue sky!

                    ROBOTIC ARM
          Look for the blue sky.

In no time Angus is encased in his shiny
new armor as the robots install the collar
section and finish it all off by placing
his helmet on him and seal him in.

                    ANGUS
          LOOK FOR THE BLUE--

His voice is muffled as the seal closes

him in.

END of FLASHBACK

EXT. PLAIN - SUNRISE

[Memories... The feel of her skin. His
hand. The small of her back. The warmth...
While Angus is thinking this, it's not
really his memory. It's a residual memory
from his DNA source.]

Angus is sleeping with his head hanging
forward in his helmet, drooling a little
bit. The sun is rising on the horizon.
Sweat sheens his skin.

Angus opens his eyes abruptly.

The rest of the soldiers are standing.
REST MODE is over. Angus watches them
as they instinctively head out in one
direction. He doesn't hear what they hear.

He gets up, shakes his head, lets out a
real yawn, looks around and then decides
to follow them.

EXT. DRY RIVERBED - EVENING

The soldiers walk along the scar of an
ancient river with Angus following them. As
they come around a butte they find...

A derelict ship. Huge. Ancient. Not human...

...and they ignore it. But Angus notices,
approaches it.

It's organic-looking, bulbous, like a
big bug, a hornet, something with black
and yellow bands and rounded shapes and
sections. He scans it.

Long antennae curve out from it, some

broken, snapped back.

Tentatively, Angus touches it. It's buried halfway into the riverbed. He's sliding his hand on the hull until he finds...

A crewmember. Petrified at the portal. Leaning against the frame of the portal. Pensive. Angus studies it. The crewmember also has armor, but not human armor. Angus turns to look to see that he's been left behind.

                    ANGUS
          Calvin? Monica? Wait for Angus.
                    (pause)
          Tycho Muhammad. Stop.

Up river, they stop. Angus listens for a response.

                    EUSTUS (O.S.)
          Who stopped us?

                    ANGUS
          Angus.

                    EUSTUS (O.S.)
          Why?

Angus looks for an answer.

                    ANGUS
          Angus found...something.

                    CALVIN (O.S.)
          What?

                    ANGUS
          Insufficient data. Wait.

Angus listens. Nothing. Angus shines his helmet lights into the portal and enters. It's dark, sand-filled, cramped. He can barely squeeze into the space.

Angus finds a handle. Tries it. Nothing.
Harder. The handle breaks. Angus looks at
the broken handle in his big augmented hand.

                    CALVIN (O.S.)
          Moving.

                    ANGUS
          What? No, wait.

Angus looks around the chamber. He has to
go. He exits.

As soon as they spot Angus approaching,
they turn and start walking. Angus strains
to catch up.

                    ANGUS
          Calvin. It was a ship.

Calvin ignores him. Angus stares at him
and looks around.

                    ANGUS
          Calvin? Calvin...! Where
          are we going?

Calvin struggles for an answer. Calvin is
suddenly SURPRISED by a recollection.

                    CALVIN
              (announcer voice)
          Forward. Secure and hold
          for PetroCom! Look for the
          blue sky.

Angus cocks his head.

                    ANGUS
          ...affirmative.

Angus follows quietly, looking back at the
receding ship.

EXT. CANYON MOUTH - DAY

The Colonial Militants arrive at another
Tower, another terraforming plant.

Sunlight slices through muddy clouds.
Patterns play on the Tower. The soldiers
sit down and wait. Angus walks around the
soldiers.

Calvin's data screen displays their current
mode: WAITING FOR SUPPLEMENTAL TROOPS
—— HRS:58:27:30 —— PLANT DEFENSE: 60 ——
ATTACKERS: 60 —— INSUFFICIENT TROOPS TO
START BATTLE! —— 20% SUPERIORITY REQUIRED
TO START BATTLE!

Angus watches Calvin as he looks at his
data screens, one after the other. Left.
Bottom left. Bottom right. Right. Top. Left
and so on.

Angus doesn't know what to make of Calvin's
mechanical quality. But, then they're all
like that. Even Angus. He stands still,
watching them for hours as they wait.

Clouds. Drizzle. Mud. Sunlight. Clouds.
Wind. Sand. Clouds. More sand. Night.

EXT. CANYON MOUTH - NIGHT

Helmet LIGHTS come on. Sand has piled on
their helmets and shoulders while they've
been waiting.

Angus' eyelids droop. [Memories... His hand
on the small of her back... CRYING.]

His eyes flutter. Open wide. Interested.

Lights crest a hill.

Pinpricks. Gradually, more appear. Three.
Then eight. Then twelve. Eighteen. Twenty-
one. Helmet lights.

Inside Calvin's helmet an alarm goes off:
BWOO-OMP. BWOO-OMP. BWOO-OMP.

Data Screen: PROXIMITY ALERT! -- PROXIMITY
ALERT! -- POSSIBLE SUPPLEMENTAL ATTACKERS!
-- PEACE CODE ^82/*6; FRIENDLY CONFIRMED --
SUPPLEMENTAL ATTACKERS: 21 35% SUPERIORITY.

Cursor BLINKING. Calvin looks out.

                    CALVIN
          This blue sky brought to you
          by GCS.

All of the Attackers hear a CHIME in their
helmets and join in chorus.

                    ATTACKERS
          This blue sky brought to you
          by GCS.

The soldiers stand up, fan out, flank the
Tower.

                    CALVIN
          Tycho Muhammad. Flank
          Furlong Midway Vectors
          twenty-seven, thirty-two,
          forty-six, fifty- five. Mark.

                    ATTACKER (O.S.)
          Mark vectors.

                    CALVIN
          Good, roger. No sign of
          detection.

                    ATTACKER (O.S.)
          True here.

Angus tries to keep up with the sudden
developments. Unlike the others, who
seem directed in their actions, he's not
included in their games.

INT. COMMAND CENTER

The screens start flashing: Optimal Battle
Condition Alert! TERRAFORMING PLANT status;
Nominal ATTacker/ DEFender balance; 81/60
-- BATTLE IMMINENT -- Engage DEFEND/ATTACK
MODES! -- AIR SUPPORT ON STAND-BY!

INT. AUTOMATED HANGAR

The Flying Vehicle's lights come on. It's
now on "ALERT."

EXT. CANYON MOUTH

The Colonial Militants Angus followed
here, and the new ones who have arrived,
automatically switch from their Neutral
Modes to Attacker status on their data
screens.

The new Attackers take up positions
according to Calvin's orders; a rough
semicircle around the Tower. Helmet lights
dot the terrain.

Angus watches nervously, unsure what to do.

                         MONICA (O.S.)
                Attacker line. Ready.
                         (pause)
                ATTACK!

Angus is surprised. Glances around. Refers
to his data screens: NEUTRAL MODE! He
checks the other Attackers' codes that he's
receiving: ATTACK MODE! He scrolls down his
options: NEUTRAL, ATTACK, DEFEND.

Angus looks around. He hesitates.

The various helmet lights close in on the
Tower, except for Angus.

Angus watches them advance. Monica

launches a rocket. Then a spray of lasers lights up the night.

Angus accesses the hid menu, scrolls down and changes "NEUTRAL" to "ATTACK." Angus follows them. He aims his laser cannon. FIRES. It hits the Tower and leaves an inconsequential bubbling black streak on the surface.

All the Attackers start firing. Launching grenades. Rockets.

INT. COMMAND CENTER

Computer screen: BATTLE COMMENCING -- ATTACK/DEFEND MODES ENGAGED! -- AIR SUPPORT ON STAND-BY! Calculating ETA.

INT. AUTOMATED HANGAR

Load lifters turn on. The Flying Vehicle waits and keeps track of the situation as well, on its data screens: DEPLOY DEFENDERS!

INT. TOWER

Defenders, again Colonial Militants like the ones outside, stand ready at the doors.

Repair crabs scurry away or hide, many in special compartments in the Colonial Militants' armor suits.

EXT. CANYON MOUTH

Light spills from the Tower as huge doors open revealing the Defenders in silhouette. Helmet lights come on.

The Defenders emerge — FIRING!

Attackers get hit. Arms. Legs. Heads. Leni

raises her cannon to fire. Gets hit by a laser. She falls.

Garth. Pump. Fires grenade. Pump. Fires another grenade.

Near the Tower, grenades stick in the sand, in front of the Defenders. The first one explodes and two Defenders are thrown back.

The second one explodes. Three Defenders are blown back.

Leni stands. Aims. Fires, bores through a Defender helmet. The Defender drops. Face down. Another Defender approaches them.

Leni shoots at the power pack on the downed Defender. The power pack EXPLODES knocking the second Defender off its feet. The Defender turns and launches a grenade.

And. Hits. Leni, square. Stuck in her armor. Five.   Four.   Three.
Two.   One.

Leni EXPLODES. Head and appendages blown in five directions. Torso blasted apart.

Five Defenders on a line. Walking. Firing lasers. Slicing across at head level.

Angus ducks. Shoots. Knocks a Defender down. Pumps. Launches grenade. It explodes. Fires again.

INT. COMMAND CENTER

Buddha calculates the Attacker/Defender balance. The Defender's are at 32% of the battle participants, then 30%. Buddha switches to another mode: LAUNCH AIR SUPPORT!

EXT. CANYON MOUTH

The Flying Vehicle cruises over the
terrain. Follows the contours. Hills roll
by underneath.

INT. FLYING VEHICLE

The Flying Vehicle's screen: CLEARANCE
WARNING!

An outcropping directly in front of the
flight path appears. The Flying Vehicle
YAWS, barely misses it.

EXT. CANYON MOUTH

Attackers and Defenders are mixing in the
battle. Fire crisscrosses between them. It
is chaos.

Angus blasts a Defender. Dead. Three beams
trap Angus in a triangle for a moment. He
spins, cuts down a Defender.

The Flying Vehicle approaches a hill. It
descends to the surface. Cuts speed. Hovers
at the crest.

INT. FLYING VEHICLE

A schematic of the hill and the battle
behind it displays on the Flying Vehicle's
screen along with: STAND BY!

EXT. CANYON MOUTH

Explosion. Angus gets knocked down. Pushes
up. Looks around. Soldiers everywhere.
Flashes, explosions. The whole canyon is
lit up by the nighttime battle.

A Defender spots Angus. Walks up to him,
aims and EXPLODES!

Angus covers himself from the shrapnel.
Defender parts.

INT. COMMAND CENTER

The computer continues to calculate the
balance of forces. Defender rank: 26%.

EXT. CANYON MOUTH

Angus gets up.

                    CALVIN (O.S.)
          All Attackers. Laser strafe
          on three.

BEEP. BEEP. BEEP. The Attackers duck.
Calvin swings his laser beam across the
battlefield. Angus watches it sweep towards
him and barely ducks in time. It knocks
down several Defenders.

Attackers shoot the remaining Defenders.
They have a clear advantage.

INT. COMMAND CENTER

Buddha calculates the balance. Defender
rank: 16%.

INT. FLYING VEHICLE

The Flying Vehicle's screen: ENGAGE AIR
SUPPORT! —— ATTACK!

EXT. CANYON MOUTH

The Flying Vehicle throttles up and over
the hill and dives into the battlefield.

INT. FLYING VEHICLE

A schematic of Attacker targets displays
on the vehicle's computer screen: MONICA
-- CALVIN -- EMPTY -- EUSTUS -- GARTH --
STRUNZ.

The Computer doesn't see Angus. Instead it
lists him as an 'empty' slot. As seen from
the air, the Attackers are in the same
order.

EXT. CANYON MOUTH

A particle beam BOLTS down. Eustus
EXPLODES, knocking Angus down.

Angus sees Eustus' lower half still
standing. Fire burns where the torso was.
Then the knees bend and the legs slowly
fall over.

Beams start taking Attackers out quickly.

Angus crawls forward. Strunz, male, 30s,
gets hit. A beam takes off his left arm.
Strunz SCREAMS and tumbles to the ground.
Angus crawls over to him.

Repair crabs appear and immediately
close off that section of armor and then
disappear. Strunz struggles to his feet.
Picks up his laser cannon with his other
arm. Resumes firing.

The Flying Vehicle fires another, direct
hit, destroying Strunz. Repair crabs scurry
from his armor, some die.

EXT. CANYON MOUTH

Angus continues crawling. The GUNFIRE
ignores him. Angus finds himself on a path
to the Tower doors, twenty meters from the
door. He gets up.

The Flying Vehicle boldly hovers meters above the battle, picking off soldiers while evading shrapnel effortlessly.

INT. COMMAND CENTER

Buddha calculates the balance: Defenders 65%.

EXT. CANYON MOUTH

More Attackers drop as the balance shifts.

Angus notices that the Tower doors are open and looks around at the battle. Attackers are falling all over while Defenders are making a minimal effort.

Angus looks up at the Flying Vehicle. It's practically sitting there. Something new happens to Angus...

He gets angry.

He aims, fires his laser and hits the Flying Vehicle. It dodges to the left, as if surprised, and instantly retaliates, hitting a Defender, instead of Angus, standing next to him. Angus watches him fall down.

INT. COMMAND CENTER

Buddha notices. Computer screen: Casualty report; 1 destroyed, 0 injured —— **ANOMALOUS TARGET**.

EXT. CANYON MOUTH

Angus sees the doors standing open. In front of him. He walks towards them.

He's nervous, this is the closest anyone has ever gotten to breaching a Tower perimeter as far as Angus knows.

Ten meters.   Five meters.
At the doors.

INT. TOWER

Inside is a white hangar.

A data screen in Angus' helmet shows
the layout of the entire Tower, which
surprises him (even he knows this should
be classified information).

The last item draws his attention, "POWER."

Another one of his data screens displays
a list of strategies and tactics: OPTIMAL
TARGET POINTS/Primary/ Power pack.

He thinks. He looks at the layout of the
Tower and makes an inquiry. His thoughts
are patched into the suit's computers, part
of the hybrid between human and machine:
INQUIRY —— next course of action?

His screens update: Default Optimal target
— Power.

A data screen immediately displays a
schematic of the ground floor leading him
to the subterranean Power sector. A HOMING
BEACON assists him as well, a hotter/colder
direction system.

INT. POWER SECTOR

Angus reaches the Power plant area and
finds the Reactor. One data screen gives
him obvious information: WARNING! —— AVOID
REACTOR SPACE! —— (Weapons prohibited
in reactor area. Sec. 846611.47. Possible
reactor damage due to...

Angus faces the Reactor. Another data
screen gives him tactical information:
PROCEED! —— Vector 227. 31 meters N/E -32.

Angus enters a large cylindrical area. A huge dynamo sits in the middle. Lights start spinning - Alarms. He scans the area.

INT. COMMAND CENTER

Computer screen: **INTRUDER ACTIVITY IN POWER SECTOR**

INT. POWER SECTOR

A schematic in Angus' helmet highlights the target. Angus makes an adjustment to his cannon. He STARES OUT.

Angus launches a grenade. CHUNK, it sticks into the Dynamo's outer casing. He launches a second grenade. CHUNK. It sticks.

Digital counters on the grenades count off.

Angus turns and leaves the Dynamo. He moves quicker than before. He can hear an AUDIO COUNTDOWN. He ascends to ground level.

Maintenance crabs come out to look. The first one to a grenade is clearly surprised. The word goes out and the crabs go into a frenzy as they scurry around the grenades, tapping, testing, probing and prodding them.

INT. GROUND LEVEL

Angus clears the ramp. Swings the cannon around. Just in case. No one is there.

He reaches the doors and stands in the center - three Defenders immediately in front of him are outside, aimed away. He aims, starting on the left. Fires. Bull's eye! Middle. Bull's eye! Right. Bull's eye!

But that was easy since they were IGNORING
HIM. He continues forward, shooting,
clearing a way. He leaves the Tower.

                    ANGUS
          Attackers! Fire in the hole!

INT. POWER SECTOR

Some of the crabs have managed to dislodge
one grenade and frantically scurry around,
trying to dispose of it.

Some want to dismantle it. Others want to
get it outside. They manage to split it
open as the digital counter reaches...ZERO.

It EXPLODES. The Dynamo casing ruptures.
The Dynamo EXPLODES in ever increasing
multiple stages. All the lights flicker and
go out.

EXT. CANYON MOUTH

Angus shudders from the SHOCK-WAVE OF
EXPLOSIONS. He steadies himself.

INT. FLYING VEHICLE

The Flying Vehicle's screen spazzes out and
goes black!

EXT. CANYON MOUTH

The Flying Vehicle pitches. External Tower
lights go out. Emergency lights come on.

INT. COMMAND CENTER

Buddha's display skews, interrupts. Then...
computer screen: EMERGENCY *** POWER
FAILURE *** EMERGENCY —— Goto BkUP Power.

INT. FLYING VEHICLE

The Flying Vehicle's screen reestablishes: SWITCHING TO ONBOARD SYSTEM.

EXT. CANYON MOUTH

The Flying Vehicle recovers altitude and stabilizes.

INT. COMMAND CENTER

Computer screen: SYSTEM DIAGNOSTIC SEARCH!! ../*MALFUNCTION* —— *SABOTAGE* —— *INTRUDER*.

Buddha figures out what happened. Computer screen: REPAIR MODE REPAIR MODE REPAIR MODE...

EXT. CANYON MOUTH

The remaining Defenders give up and return to the Tower. It's no longer a battle, it's REPAIR MODE.

Angus turns. Fires at them. He drops two. Three.

The rest of the Attackers stop shooting and stand by. Angus notices them and is confused.

INT. TOWER

Pressure and heat gauges quickly drop and rise.

Computer screen: EMERGENCY EMERGENCY EMERGENCY **FULL GENERATOR FAILURE** **REACTOR COOLANT POWER FAILURE** **REACTOR COOLANT PRESSURE LOSS** DANGER DANGER...

SIRENS go off. Red lights spin. KLAXONS.

Codes.

EXT. CANYON MOUTH

Angus has the data on one of his screens.
He suddenly realizes what it means as he
does a double-take.

                    ANGUS (O.S.)
          All Attackers,...evacuate field!

Monica's data screens indicate the current
situation as well: **Evacuate all NON-
ESSENTIAL personnel! CORRECTION **REACTOR
EMERGENCY! **EVACUATE ALL PERSONNEL!
**REACTOR FAILURE!

Monica stares at the screen not knowing
what it means.

                    ANGUS (O.S.)
          All Attackers, evacuate field!
          The reactor is going to
          detonate!

She doesn't get it. She looks up. The Tower
emergency lights are all on. Angus runs
towards her.

                    MONICA
          Tycho Muhammad. Calvin?
          Confirm situation analysis.

                    CALVIN (O.S.)
          ...Stand by, Monica.

Calvin doesn't get it either.

                    ANGUS (O.S.)
          Evacuate field. Reactor
          emergency. All Attackers,
          evacuate field. The reactor
          is going to detonate!

Angus passes them, running away from the
tower. Monica is persuaded by dint of his

exuberant example.

                    MONICA
          Code nine, nine, nine!
          Emergency. Reactor. Failure.
          Evacuate coordinates three-
          seven-three, six, oh-oh,
          eighteen-two-two and nine-
          five-one. Mark.

Monica turns to flee. Calvin hesitates.

Some Attackers start to turn. Others
hesitate. Unsure. About half of the
remaining Attackers are now fleeing.

Calvin turns to follow them. Stops. Turns
back. Stops. Turns again. Confused.
Finally, he runs after them.

Huge armor is hard to move. Nonetheless
they move quickly. They climb a ridge
leading out of the canyon. The other
Attackers finally get it.

INT. TOWER

Heat gauges rise rapidly. Pressures drop
fast.

INT. FLYING VEHICLE

The Flying Vehicle fires on the retreating
Attackers.

The Flying Vehicle's screen changes to:
**EVACUATE AIRSPACE! **RADIATION EMERGENCY!
**EVACUATE AIRSPACE!

EXT. CANYON MOUTH

The Flying Vehicle stops shooting,
throttles up and veers in a straight line
away from the Tower.

Now some Defenders - very few - try to
flee.

INT. TOWER

Heat and pressure gauges hit <u>Max</u>.

EXT. CANYON MOUTH

Angus is out in front with Monica. Calvin
is close behind with the other Attackers.

The ridge crest is in sight. Thirty meters.
Twenty. Ten.   Over it. Angus stumbles.
Falls. Rolls down the slope.

Calvin clears it. The others follow
clumsily.

The last Attackers and Defenders running
as fast as they can. Nearing the ridge.

The Tower is now a

                    WHITE FLASH

The reactor has EXPLODED. The BLAST
incinerates everything within sight in
the Canyon mouth. The last few Attackers
and the few Defenders to understand the
situation are VAPORIZED in mid-step.

Those over the side of the ridge are saved
from the heat.

But the shockwave lifts the fleeing
Attackers and Defenders and hurls them.
Some are dismembered by the force. Others
are smashed like empty cans.

Angus, Monica, Calvin, all get thrown
like toys. They slam, tumble and roll to

painful stops at the bottom of the ridge.

[Memories again... The gloved hand. The
tear on his cheek. CRYING.]

The wind hurled by the shockwave covers
them with tons of sand and debris as a
roiling mushroom cloud climbs into the sky
where the Tower used to be. It illuminates
the area for some time and then gradually
dims...

Darkness covers the battleground.

EXT. CANYON MOUTH - MORNING

A huge black-stained crater is where the
Tower was. Everything smolders. The wind
sprays sand.

An audio signal: HOO, TIK. HOO, TIK. Angus
is unconscious. His eyes move about under
his lids.

Inside Angus' helmet is almost pitch black.
He opens his eyes. Slowly. More lights come
on. His faceplate is rust colored. Sand?
Buried in sand?

He looks at his data screens. Reads.
Thinks. Scrolls down menus. Stops at
"PROXIMITY SCAN." Data Screen: Monica;
Calvin; etc.

                    ANGUS
          Monica?
                    (pause)
          Calvin?

He scrolls back to "DAMAGE INVENTORY."
That displays his suit layout: Intact. He
scrunches his eyes shut. GRUNTS.

A pile of sand moves. An "L" shape rises
from the sand, an arm, a hand. Feels
about. Pushes down. Lifts up. Sand pours

off Angus. He pushes up with his other
arm. Climbs out from the sand, sits up and
slowly looks around.

Footprints. Tracks.

Another pile. He crawls over. Brushes away
sand. Uncovers Monica's battered helmet.
The faceplate is intact. Her eyes are
closed. He scans her: Monica — 85.356338%
rehab.

Her eyes are moving under her lids.
STRANGE. He tugs on her, rolls her over.
Small lights go on in her helmet. Sand
pours off. Her suit seems intact. Angus
sits back.

                    ANGUS
          Buddha? Angus reporting
          ninety-nine point nine,
          nine, nine, seven, three
          percent rehab. Ready.

Nothing. Thinks. He looks at one of his
data screens: BUDDHA Telemetry Network
Inquiry — Why no response?

He waits. Data Screen: DAMAGE INVENTORY!
Telemetry broken. Malfunction in ENET-
1 microprocessor. **No transmission of
recognition codes to recognize parties
in communication. Required for data
recognition.

He tries again.

                    ANGUS
          Buddha. Angus reporting
          ninety-nine point nine,
          nine, nine, seven, three
          percent rehab. Ready.

Nothing. Angus looks at Monica. Stands up.
Walks around. He studies the tracks around
them. Apparently some soldiers went back

on-line and left.

He walks to the ridge and looks back at the Tower. Black smears are where soldiers had been, radiating from ground zero.

A proximity alert AUDIO SIGNAL goes off, startling Angus. He turns, looks for the source. His suit shows him trajectories and a reticle, projected on his faceplate, showing him where to look. But he's caught off-guard.

Finally he focuses and sees a dot on the horizon. Data Screen: Approaching Colonial Militant Transmitting Peace code ^82/*60 FRIENDLY CONFIRMED!

Angus perks up and squints at the far off figure. Data Screen: IDENTIFICATION — ELDON 0821.

                    ANGUS
                 (to himself)
          ...Eldon...

He steps forward, reflexively.

                    ANGUS
          Greetings, Eldon.

There's no response. Instead Angus watches ELDON approach, gradually, slowly, step-by-step. Angus returns to Monica's side.

                    ANGUS
          Greetings, Eldon zero
          eight, two one.

Nothing. Angus watches the soldier continue to approach. Dust and heat waves obscure him. He's walking directly towards Angus, gradually becoming bigger.

Closer. Clearer. It takes some time.

Eldon gets close enough for Angus to read

his markings. His armor is clean and polished. Right off the assembly line, big PETROCOM logos throughout.

Eldon's data screens show a <u>layout of Angus</u>. He's definitely there, in front of him — a whole list of physical attributes.

But no name. No received codes. No "PEACE" codes. No "HOSTILE" codes. Therefore Eldon ignores him as he walks up to Angus.

He stops because of Monica, and looks down at her. His data screen shows a layout of Monica, prone, on the ground: Monica — 85.356338% rehab.

                    ANGUS
          Greetings!

Angus blinks. Eldon is an exact replica of Angus, only younger. He's barely a young man, a teenager still.

Still nothing. Angus touches Eldon on the arm. Eldon turns and looks at Angus.

                    ELDON
          Who are you?

                    ANGUS
          Angus. Seven eight, seven three.

Eldon blinks at him. Angus stares at Eldon's face. It's smooth and rosy whereas Angus is creased, drawn and tanned. It's like looking into a strange mirror of youth.

                    ANGUS
          Angus. Seven eight, seven three.

Angus touches him again. It's the only way to get him to address him.

                    ELDON
          You are not...identified.

                    ANGUS
          Negative. No that's not
          true. Angus sev...Angus!

Eldon looks at Monica again. Angus touches
him again. Eldon looks at Angus, pauses,
thinking, and concludes.

                    ELDON
          You are not identified.

                    ANGUS
          Angus! Angus!

Eldon turns and continues in the same
direction.

                    ANGUS
          Wait. Stop. Eldon!

Eldon ignores him.

                    ANGUS
          Where are you going?

Eldon turns dramatically and
enthusiastically says, as if he were in a
television commercial,...

                    ELDON
          Forward! Secure and hold
          for PetroCom. Look for the
          blue sky!

Angus is exasperated.

                    ANGUS
          Wait. Don't go...Eldon!
          Don't go. Don't leave.

Angus watches Eldon walk away and just
as gradually become a dot again on the
opposite horizon.

Monica's data screen indicates her diagnostic procedure has stalled: Monica — 85.356338% rehab.

Angus turns back to her. He looks at his own data screens. A cursor blinks insistently.

                    ANGUS
                  (nervous)
          Monica.

Another of his screens displays: Inquiry — Estimated time to 100% rehab.

The answer he gets is: REPAIR MODE ERROR. Repair routine CANNOT PROCEED as directed. Start again or refer to external diagnostics.

                    ANGUS
          Monica? Monica?

Angus kneels next to her. Looks at her face. Her eyes are still moving under her lids. He watches her for a while.

He looks up. Eldon is gone. Not even a dot on the horizon anymore. But, his TRACKS TRAIL behind him.

Angus resumes looking at Monica. An expression crosses her face. Weird. He crouches closer to look. He watches. Another expression. Far and few between. But he watches for them. He's astonished.

Data Screen: Inquiry — Movements, face?

His answer is: Involuntary muscle contractions due to peripheral cerebral activity during ROD (read only dream) states. No significance. All critical and/or Hi-Cap brain activity directed by BUDDHA or built-in sub-directories.

Another expression. The corners of Monica's mouth rise. A faint smile. Angus stares at her, <u>watching someone dream</u>, for real, for the <u>first time in his life</u>.

He reaches out and touches her helmet. He looks up again at the tracks Eldon left. Studies them. Follows them.

Horizon to Monica. And. From Monica. To... the <u>first tracks</u> Eldon left.

Angus stands and stares at the first tracks then at Monica.

Hesitant. Unsure. He looks all around. At the sky. The sun. The twin neighboring moons. The ground.

Angus turns and follows the first tracks to look for Eldon's origin.

EXT. PLAIN - AFTERNOON

Eldon's footprints curve around a huge wreckage half buried in the sand. It's another huge ship, human technology, a transport. On the side is GeoConSo, Geo-Consolidated.

Angus approaches the wreckage. Eldon had completely circumvented it and continued on his original course.

It's broken, nose here, storage and propulsion about two hundred meters away. Laser scars are all over it, especially on the engines.

Angus stares at it.

INT. NOSE SECTION

The floor is buckled from crash damage. Indirect light from a tear in the fuselage fills the area. Angus struggles forward and finds the bridge.

Four pilots sit in a helm pod, surrounded by the space of the nose section. The pilots wear GeoConSo spacesuits.

The human bodies look tiny compared to Angus in his oversized Colonial Militant armor. Angus peers into a faceplate. A skull grins back at him. It's black and shiny, almost polished. <u>Very old</u>.

INT. AFT SECTION

Angus climbs in. He finds all of the storage bays, empty. He finds a ladder to the other levels.

INT. UPPER LEVEL

Angus finds a large room. In the corner is <u>a body in a pressure suit</u>. Another grinning, blackened, desiccated skull. Sand covers everything.

He moves over to a computer terminal. There are lights still on!

He brushes sand off. Someone put a sticker on the console that says: HAVE A NICE SOLAR CYCLE! There's too much sand. Angus looks around.

He goes over to the dead crewman, takes a cannister off his back, it's empty. He grabs the second one and goes back to the console.

With one hand he opens the valve and sprays pressurized air over the console and blows the dust away...

Revealing more stickers, placed by philosophical crew: ARE YOU WORKING TO

LIVE, OR LIVING TO WORK?, THIS IS THE
FIRST SOLAR CYCLE OF THE REST OF YOUR LIFE
and PROCESS LOVE, NOT WAR.

He sits down at the terminal. The screen
is pale, faded. It has a red "COLLISION
ALERT" screen on it, blinking.

Angus touches a key. The screen changes.
But the red alert, burnt into the screen,
remains seen over the menu.

Angus pulls a cable out of his suit and
plugs into a standard jack on the console.
Now the main menu from the ship's console
is also on Angus' data screens.

                    SHIP COMPUTER
          Hi, Angus seven eight, seven
          three. May I help you?

Angus is stunned by the voice recognizing
him.

It's the SHIP'S COMPUTER speaking, a
business-like but pleasant female voice. He
moves his lips, not knowing what to say.

                    SHIP COMPUTER
          You have successfully patched
          into my data port. Unless
          otherwise indicated, I will
          upload primary inventory
          directories in ten seconds.

Angus doesn't know what to do. All of the
screens start flashing as they transfer
data to him.

The lights reflect off his faceplate as he
absorbs more and more data. His eyes open
wider and wider. His big armored hands
twitch as screens flash by faster and
faster.

His head starts to pull back, away from

the console.

Screens flashing, his eyes roll back into his head. He's taking on too much data too quickly. His hands and arms twitch abortively and repetitively.

Data screens: ^^ SYSTEM OVERLOAD ^^.

                    SHIP COMPUTER
          Primary inventory
          directories successfully
          uploaded. What would you
          like to know?

Angus passes out.

LATER

Angus blinks and looks around. He seems hungover. He stays put for a while studying his surroundings.

The data screens show him an interface indicating all of the directories on the different available hard drives.

Angus wakes up some more with an idea in mind.

                    SHIP COMPUTER
          Alright. Accessing Flight
          Record. Flight Record.
          What would you like to
          know about Flight Record?

His thoughts, his questions, are immediately read by the ship's computer who answers them. His data screens show the pertinent files and any video images available.

                    SHIP COMPUTER
          Flight Record, GeoConSo Transport
          five four three zero.

                    (pause)
          Zero five hundred, <u>thirty</u>:
          Departure from GeoConSo
          Plant 59. Mission, return
          home (GcX three-two
          double-u three). Nominal
          flight performance.
          Destination, GeoConSo
          Largo Earth Station 33, to
          GeoConSo, Earth.
                    (pause)
          Zero five hundred,
          <u>thirty-five</u>: Engage enemy
          aircraft. No escort.
                    (pause)
          Zero five hundred, <u>thirty-</u>
          <u>five</u>: Mayday transmission
          to GeoConSo Plant 59 and
          GeoConSo Largo Earth
          Station. Evasive action.
                    (pause)
          Zero five hundred, <u>thirty-</u>
          <u>seven</u>: Direct hits on
          starboard engines. Heavy
          damage.
                    (pause)
          Zero five hundred, <u>thirty-</u>
          <u>eight</u>: Engine failure. Loss
          of flight worthiness.
                    (pause)
          Zero five hundred, <u>thirty-</u>
          <u>nine</u>: Crash. All (ten)
          crewmembers expired. Zero
          cargo. End flight record.

Angus blinks, another question occurs to
him.

                    SHIP COMPUTER
          Mission: Return Home.
          Departure, solar time——
                    (interrupting)
          Accessing final log.
          GeoConSo Transport five

>   four three zero attacked
>   by Petrocom escort ships.
>   No rescue/salvage attempt——

One data screen shows footage from the
ship's cameras of the attack, the crash and
the subsequent hours and days.

Angus scrolls up to a line item. Console
screen: MISSION; Return Home <u>GcX32w3</u>.

>   SHIP COMPUTER
>   Mission profile, Return
>   Home. GeoConSo five four
>   three zero was on return
>   flight to GeoConSo Largo
>   Earth Station, GeoConSo,
>   Earth, according to order
>   GcX three-two double-u
>   three——

One data screen shows the transport taking
off. The ship's computer responds with
another screen: MISSION DETAIL — <u>GcX32w3</u>;
Return Home. Recall all transport and non-
planetary equipment. <u>GCS Order 8685.335</u>.

>   SHIP COMPUTER
>   Order GcX three-two
>   double-u three, Return
>   Home, according to <u>GCS</u>
>   <u>Order eight six eight five</u>
>   <u>dot three three five</u>——
>   (interrupting)
>   Accessing <u>GCS Order eight</u>
>   <u>six eight five dot three</u>
>   <u>three five</u>.
>   (pause)
>   <u>GCS Order eight six</u>
>   <u>eight five dot three</u>
>   <u>three five</u>; All movable
>   personnel and equipment
>   recalled in compliance
>   with <u>CANCELLATION</u> of
>   Terraforming operation on

                    CEM.4 (A Centauri system
                    one eight seven).

Angus thinks for a long while.

                         SHIP COMPUTER
                    Standing by--
                         (interrupting)
                    May I help you--
                         (interrupting)
                    What would you like to
                    know--

Console screen: CANCELLATION of
Terraforming operation.

                         SHIP COMPUTER
                    GCS Comm. Seven seven
                    seven eight seven four
                    eight. Last Communication:
                    Terraforming Operation
                    CANCELLATION. All GeoConSo
                    terraforming operations on
                    CEM.4 have been cancelled.
                    Current transports are
                    redirected--
                         (interrupting)
                    For further information I
                    recommend the following
                    files.

Angus contemplates the current screen: GCS
COMM. 7778743: *GcX32w* *GCS Order 8685.33*
Evac *Plant Shutdown* *GCS Annual Report*

                         SHIP COMPUTER
                    Accessing Annual Report.

Angus' faceplate goes opaque as the annual
report is projected on it.

Another voice, the ANNUAL REPORT voice, an
appealing woman's voice, reads the copy of
the Annual Report with perfect tone and
manner. The accompanying video images are
beautiful and very colorful.

                    ANNUAL REPORT VOICE
          The GeoConSolidated Annual
          Report, Two Thousand
          Three Hundred Twenty-Two.
          Reaching to the stars for
          a better life on Earth.

It's designed to be seen by <u>shareholders</u>,
<u>not soldiers</u>.

                    ANNUAL REPORT VOICE
          Contents: Letter To Our
          Shareholders, Annual
          Report, Statements of
          Operations, Balance Sheets,
          Assets, Liabilities and
          Shareholders' Equity, and
          Future   pla—
                    (interrupting)
          Letter To Our
          Shareholders.

A video begins of an enthusiastic and
smiling pudgy white man in a suit and
tie, the GCS CEO, 50s. His name, WESLEY
FOEGHAARD, is superimposed on the image.

Smiles are new to Angus. His face
inadvertently mimics one. He's never seen a
man in his fifties, smiling.

                    WESLEY FOEGHAARD
          Dear...Angus seven eight,
          seven three: I am very
          happy to say that last
          year proved to be——

Angus stops the video and stares at this
strange phenomenon. This is the oldest man
he's ever seen, dressed in the oddest way.
A portion replays.

                    WESLEY FOEGHAARD
          I am very happy to say——
                    (rewind)
          I am very happy——

                    (rewind)
          I am——
                    (rewind)
          I——

Angus stares at him.

                    ANGUS
          ...I...

...and into space, thinking.

                    WESLEY FOEGHAARD
          I am very happy to say
          that last year proved
          to be a great year for
          GeoConSolidated, witnessing
          an 89 percent increase
          in overall operations,
          up from our 65 percent
          increase the year before.
          Net sales for the year
          ended December 31 Twenty-
          three, twenty-two——

Angus' faceplate and his data screens
are coordinated in a startling multimedia
symphony, illustrating the information of
the annual report.

According to Angus' interest, as with the
ship's computer, the annual report moves on
to other items.

                    ANNUAL REPORT VOICE
               (interrupting)
          Moving on.

                    WESLEY FOEGHAARD
          ...continue from changes
          the Company instituted ten
          years ago. Seeking strategic
          opportunities and new product
          developments to enhance the
          Company's growth——

                    ANNUAL REPORT VOICE
                         (interrupting)
          Moving on.

                    WESLEY FOEGHAARD
          ...Sometimes, to continue
          healthy, one must clear away
          old growth and make room
          for the new. Some operations
          deemed unprofitable have
          been phased out; the Jovian
          Asteroid Belt Station, the
          Great Alaskan Oil Fields
          and several outer world
          operations. These moves have
          contributed to the Company's
          profitability--

Angus watches video snippets of the Jovian
Asteroid Belt Station, the Great Alaskan
Oil Fields and the outer world operations.

The outer world operations look a lot like
the planet and operation Angus knows,
terraforming plants and towers. Wesley's
margarine smile gets interrupted.

                    ANNUAL REPORT VOICE
                         (interrupting)
          Moving on. Annual Report.
          An overview on GeoConSo's
          operations. Fossil fuels
          and mining throughout the
          known universe.

The introduction to the Annual Report is
a montage with lots of glitzy pictures
of happy people working and playing.
Apparently, GeoConSo is making lots of
people happy, smiles everywhere.

A man and a woman and smaller versions of
both of them, children, all smiling, on a
deck, part of a big white structure, a house.
Lots of windows and artwork on the walls.

The four people, <u>the family</u>, look at the planets in the sky. In <u>the blue sky</u>. Angus stares at the blue sky. He's used to a sky the color of rust.

Now the family is on a beautiful beach. The woman is wearing a bikini. Angus stares at her body...

Memories... His hand on the small of her back...

His huge armored hand twitches.

              ANNUAL REPORT VOICE
      The work that GeoConSo does
      makes all of this possible.

The annual report runs down a list of accomplishments as shown.

              ANNUAL REPORT VOICE
      New refinery techniques
      perfected by GeoConSo.

Silhouettes and sunsets...

              ANNUAL REPORT VOICE
      Lunar operations.

Working personnel. Structures on Earth's moon...

              ANNUAL REPORT VOICE
      The gas giants; energy
      research.

Everyone's smiling stupidly, orbiting Jupiter and Saturn!

              ANNUAL REPORT VOICE
      Military research and
      development.

Gung-ho and technoid photographs...

                    ANNUAL REPORT VOICE
          Deep space operations.

This stops Angus cold.

It's a picture of a shiny, brand new
colonial militant, not soldered and welded
together from salvaged pieces, but factory-
made.

He's heroic, towering, on a desolate planet
in a binary system; two suns in the
background. He looks like a younger Calvin.
There are more militants behind him.

In the background, peeking through clouds,
is a tower. As he looks at it, the annual
report captions it (kind of like pop-ups in
computers of today).

                    ANNUAL REPORT VOICE
          Terraforming Oxygenation
          Plants.

Angus is transfixed...

                    ANNUAL REPORT VOICE
          Terraforming Plants and
          Refineries are placed on
          dead planets with oxygen
          rich soils in an effort to
          return them to Earth-like
          splendor. In a short time
          these planets are ready
          for use in our massive
          colonization effort.

An animated diagram shows how the Towers
take oxygen in the planet's soil, convert
it to gas and pump it into the atmosphere.
The animation shows the rebirth of the
entire planet, sped up for our edification.

                    ANNUAL REPORT VOICE
          GCS's Colonial Militia helps
          secure these planets for

exclusive use by GCS brand
colonies. Against competing
companies like PetroCom,
InfraSpace, ExxoCon, and
others, the Colonial Militia
graciously provides an
invaluable service.

The annual report shows shiny happy
Colonial Militants, by the thousands,
lining up to board transport ships, much
like this one.

All of the faces he sees are the same
faces he's seen in all of his battles,
Calvin, Eustus, Strunz, Leni, Monica, and
his own.

The animation shows a sanitized version of
the massive colonization effort mentioned
before.

Landing on a desolate planet, claiming it,
as shown by an animated field of color
with the GeoConSo logo spreading over the
planet, obliterating the competitors' logos,
and hundreds of towers now working away,
terraforming this planet into a beautiful
cousin of Earth.

                    ANNUAL REPORT VOICE
          Six operations have so
          far proven to be great
          successes——

The image of thousands of Towers spewing
vapors is almost identical to 20th century
footage of factories polluting Earth's
atmosphere, but these are making lethal
atmospheres breathable.

Another picture shows a Tower with a puffy
white plume growing out the top, with
green grass and trees growing around the
plant and refinery, framed by a brilliant
blue sky.

The shiny new Colonial Militant stands triumphant, without his helmet, in this new world.

                    ANNUAL REPORT VOICE
                       (interrupting)
              Colonial Militants are men
              and women specially trained
              for their valued service.

FLASHBACK:

Angus remembers the Defender, <u>Roach</u>, with his helmet torn off, <u>breathing the atmosphere on this planet, screaming</u>.

END of FLASHBACK:

                    ANNUAL REPORT VOICE
              Colonial Militants are
              administered in their
              combat activities through
              the help of our GCS
              Systems Hologrammatical
              ONYX computer arrays.
              As needed, ONYX systems
              present to the Colonial
              Militants as divine
              figures, an identity
              that brings out the most
              commitment and dedication,
              such as Buddha, Muhammad,
              Vishnu, Jesus, and others.
                       (pause)
              With their Militia
              suits and the telemetry
              assistance of their
              central supervisory
              computer they combat
              competing companies. Only
              the best computer is good
              enough for our Colonial
              Militia; the GCS Systems
              Hologrammatical ONYX.

Angus' attention returns to a picture
of a particularly large Tower complex,
apparently with "Buddha," the ONYX computer
inside.

                    ANNUAL REPORT VOICE
          When strategic alliances
          are formed ONYX systems
          can easily and immediately
          end bellicose operations
          and form cooperative
          ventures, allowing
          for better combat
          administration——

A picture of a dish antenna. Computer
animation of a satellite in orbit.

                    ANNUAL REPORT VOICE
                    (interrupting)
          ...Our best orbital
          satellite model, the
          OS17, is used to keep
          all Colonial Militia in
          constant contact.

Buddha sends the phrase "This blue sky
brought to you by GCS." on a friendly
animated lighting bolt to the satellite
which then sends it to the waiting shiny
new Colonial Militant, which seems to start
up and move into action.

The soldier smiles and waves his huge
armored hand.

                    SHINY NEW COLONIAL
                    MILITANT
          This blue sky brought to
          you by GCS.

                    ANGUS
          ...look for the blue sky...

Angus' jaw clenches. He glances at the ARE
YOU WORKING TO LIVE, OR LIVING TO WORK

sticker. Minutes, perhaps hours go by...

LATER

The annual report is droning on with Angus moping.

> ANNUAL REPORT VOICE
> Some operations have
> been cancelled due to
> poor profit projections.
> Planetary research shows
> that CAL.6 (A Centauri
> system two one eight)
> would require a larger
> effort than GCS is
> prepared for at this time.
> CEM.4 (A Centauri system
> one eight seven) a long
> and particularly difficult
> operation has been
> cancelled due to heavy
> initial investment costs.

Angus blinks and perks up. The annual report repeats herself.

> ANNUAL REPORT VOICE
> CEM.4 (A Centauri system
> one eight seven) a long
> and particularly difficult
> operation has been
> cancelled due to heavy
> initial investment costs.

He gulps. Another window and menu calls up the mission profile.

> SHIP COMPUTER
> Mission Profile——
>
> (interrupting)
> Moving on. GCS Order eight
> six eight five dot three
> three five;... CANCELLATION
> of Terraforming operation

                on CEM.4 (A Centauri
                system one eight seven)...

The "CEM.4 (A.Centauri system 187)" on
the mission profile window and "CEM.4
(A.Centauri system 187)" on the annual
report screen match. It is the same planet
Angus has lived and fought on his whole
life.

Angus opens a third window, goes back to
the GCS Comm. 7778743 Last Communication
menu.

Console screen: GCS COMM. 7778743* *GcX32w*
GCS Order 8685.33 *Evac* *Plant Shutdown*
GCS Annual Report

He accesses "*Evac*."

                         SHIP COMPUTER
                Evacuation Order:
                Terraforming Operation
                planet CEM.4 (in the Alpha
                Centauri, system one eight
                seven) is to be evacuated
                of all transport and non-
                planetary equipment and
                personnel. All Colonial
                Militia and Terraforming
                Plants are losses and to
                be left behind.

Angus thinks a question. The Ship
Computer's words chip away at Angus'
expression.

                         SHIP COMPUTER
                Cancel: One, verb: to give
                up something previously
                arranged or agreed on.
                Call off, Drop, Scrub,
                End, Terminate, Annul,
                Invalidate,
                         (pause)
                Two, verb: to eliminate or

                    neutralize with or as if
                    with a stroke of the pen.
                    Erase, Annul, Black out,
                    Blot out, Delete——

Another question occurs to him. These
words continue to erode what little
confidence and self-esteem exists in him.

                    SHIP COMPUTER
               ...As in garbage, refuse,
               debris, trash, unwanted
               materials, discard.
               Two, Phrase: forgotten,
               overlooked, negl—

Angus looks back at the annual report. The
annual report repeats herself again.

                    ANNUAL REPORT VOICE
                    (interrupting)
               ...operation has been
               cancelled due to heavy
               initial investment costs.

Angus' expression flutters between
unfamiliar thoughts and pains.

                    SHIP COMPUTER
               Would you like anything
               else, Angus seven eight,
               seven three?

Angus snaps out of it and seems to glare
at the ship's computer.

EXT. PLAIN - NIGHT

Angus walks away from the crash site. The
neighboring twin planets are waxing, at
a quarter now. His helmet lights are on,
shining two white ovals on his tracks back
to Monica.

Angus has an expression of deep

concentration, or anger. The HISSING wind pelts him from the side with sand. On the long walk, Angus stares at the time counter again.

> ANGUS
> Seconds, minutes, hours, days, weeks, months, years. Seconds, minutes, hours, days, weeks, months, years...

EXT. CANYON MOUTH

Angus is a set of tiny twin lights in the violet expanse, following his tracks up the ridge, to Monica, partially buried in the sand. He kneels beside her, scans her.

Data Screen: Monica: 85.356338% rehab. Life signs: Stable.

He drags her out of the sand, looks at her through her faceplate. The violet light makes her scary looking. His helmet lights wash away the violet. Her eyes are still moving. She's drooled a bit.

He pulls a cable from his back and attaches it to a metal loop on Monica's suit. He does the same on the other side, takes a step away and the cables winch her, drag her up and onto his back. He scoots under her weight, then stands up.

He tests his balance; a huge Colonial soldier with an equally huge burden. He starts walking, tracing his tracks back to the crash site.

INT. REPAIR ROOM, GEOCONSO TRANSPORT 5430

Door opens to the outside. Angus drags Monica in and over to an angled table the shape of a soldier. He connects himself to the console.

                    SHIP COMPUTER
          Hi, Angus seven eight, seven
          three. May I help you?

This startles him again. He places her on
the table and connects her computer link
to it.

                    SHIP COMPUTER
          Hi, Monica two four, eight
          eight. May I help you?

Angus accesses "environmental control."

                    SHIP COMPUTER
          Pressurizing repair room, standby.

He opens a vent in his helmet. Tests the
air. He sneezes repeatedly, but it's okay.

                    SHIP COMPUTER
          Bless you!

He's never sneezed before, not that he can
remember. Angus looks at Monica's face,
then he sits down at the terminal.

                    SHIP COMPUTER
          Starting repair mode diagnosis.
                    (pause)
          Monica two four, eight
          eight is eighty-five percent
          functional. Automated repair
          mode cannot proceed due to
          an error, error two eight——
                    (interrupting)
          Locating malfunction.
                    (pause)
          CMX 2B microprocessor is
          burnt out. Would you like
          to replace——

Angus blinks a thought at the ship's
computer.

                    SHIP COMPUTER
          Replacing.

The table comes to life as repair crabs
come out of it, Monica's suit and the
walls.

Two of them open a hatch on her back. A
tiny board pops out. One crab plucks out a
chip. The other replaces it with a new one.
The board slides back in.

                    SHIP COMPUTER
          CMX 2B replaced and
          operative.

Angus looks at Monica on the table.

                    SHIP COMPUTER
          Start repair mode, automatic
          or manual?
                    (pause)
          Manual.

The computer runs down all of the
components and lists them allowing Angus
to decide what gets repaired. Repair
crabs scurry all over Monica. He okays
everything until it gets to the ENET-1
MICROPROCESSOR.

                    SHIP COMPUTER
          Reset?

Angus shakes his head, no.

                    SHIP COMPUTER
          Disabling ENET-1 micro-
          processor will prevent
          telemetry control by Buddha
          of Monica two four,——
                    (interrupting)
          ENET-1 microprocessor is
          disabled.

They continue the rest of the repair

routine.

INT. LABORATORY - (FLASHBACK)

Crying, a toddler in an incubator. Blurry shapes. A rubber gloved hand, finger reaches down and wipes away a tear. The toddler blinks at being touched. The hand lingers...

Angus as a boy (9). He watches as other children walk along a metal corridor. There are lights, sounds. The whole place is a scary machine.

LATER

Angus is older (13), walking along the metal corridor in a line of other adolescents, all in grey jumpsuits.

RECREATION ROOM: Angus in a wire frame version of the Colonial Militia suits. Training. A whole row of kids are training.

DORMITORIES: Young Angus sleeping. All of them in capsules, similar to coffins, have caps on linking them to a computer; Hypno-learning.

SIMULATOR: Young Angus in target practice with an apparatus on his arm and head; Laser sighting.

ASSEMBLY ROOM: Young Angus (16) steps up to a platform. A machine picks him up and "builds" an armor suit around his fetal pose.

Finally three cables are fastened to the back of his head. Sparks. Pain. Then the helmet.

RECEIVING AREA: Huge doors OPEN. Outside is an arid plain.

EXT. PLAIN - DAY (FLASHBACK)

Young Angus looks up at the sky for the
very first time as he steps outside. He's
astonished by the sight.

But, computer buffers dampen his curiosity.

His face literally shuts down...from the
astonished expression he initially had. He
turns his attention to the plain and sets
out to wander.

EXT. BATTLEGROUND (FLASHBACK)

Young Angus is in a battle. Mayhem
surrounds him.

The Defenders, with help from the Flying
Vehicle, neutralize the Attackers.

Some are instantly destroyed. Smoke is
everywhere, smoke that drifts away as
the battle subsides, smoke that clears to
reveal a <u>tower</u>.

This tower is huge. And out of the top.
Nothing. No converted oxygen pumped into
the atmosphere. No white vapor. No blue
sky.

AFTER THE BATTLE: the field is littered
with the injured, dying and dead. Faces in
pain, crying out. Angus watches.

END of FLASHBACK

INT. REPAIR ROOM, GEOCONSO TRANSPORT 5430

Angus is asleep with his helmet off. He
startles awake, disturbed. He's sitting
against a wall.

He stands and sees Monica. Her helmet is
also off. She too is bald. She is in a

chair in rest mode. Angus shakes the sleep
out of his head and thinks.

He notices something and gets closer to
her. Her face twitches, Monica is dreaming.
Tears are streaming down her face. He's
fascinated and slowly reaches out to touch
one.

His huge armored hand carefully touches
her face. He can "feel" it through his
armor and he reacts slightly. The situation
makes him self-conscious and he snaps out
of it. He steps back as she wakes.

Incongruously he launches into a good
mimicry of the ship computer's enthusiasm.

                    ANGUS
          Hi, Monica two four, eight
          eight.
                    (pause)
          Where are we going?

She gapes at him, recognizing her
designation, her name. But, she doesn't
recognize him.

                    MONICA
          Forward. Secure and hold
          for PetroCom.

She didn't think, she just said it. Angus
stares at her.

                    ANGUS
                    (whispered)
          Look for the blue sky...

                    MONICA
          Buddha. Monica reporting
          one hundred percent rehab.
          Ready.

No response. She periodically looks at
Angus.

                    MONICA
          Buddha. Monica reporting
          one hundred percent rehab.
          Ready. Respond.

                    ANGUS
          Your ENET-1 is disabled.

She heard what he said and seems to
corroborate that with her own data screens.

                    ANGUS
          It controls transmissions
          with Buddha.

She checks that.

                    ANGUS
          Buddha will not respond.

After consideration she looks at him.

                    ANGUS
          You were damaged in the
          last battle.

She considers their surroundings and that
her helmet is off.

                    ANGUS
          A GeoConSo Transport ship.

She gives the place another look.

                    MONICA
          ...There are no transport
          ships.

                    ANGUS
          This one is...old...crashed.

Monica nods almost imperceptibly. Angus
walks over.

                    ANGUS
          Look.

                    SHIP COMPUTER
          May I help you——Accessing.

Angus shows her everything he's learned,
with help from the ship computer.

She watches intently. He shows her
everything he learned from the GeoConSo
annual report and the Flight Record. He
gives her a lot to think about.

                    SHIP COMPUTER
          ...Against competing
          companies like PetroCom,
          InfraSpace, ExxoCon and
          others the Colonial
          Militia graciously provides
          an...

He stares at Monica.

                    ANGUS
          What happened to GeoConSo,
          InfraSpace and ExxoCon?

Monica thinks, instead of responding. He
looks into her eyes. She looks back at him
without any reaction.

                    ANGUS
          Monica two four, eight eight.
          What are you...doing here?

Monica stares at him.

                    ANGUS
          What is your mission?

                    MONICA
          Secure and hold for
          PetroCom.

                    ANGUS
          What is that?

Monica stares at him, but this time she's

thinking more.

                    ANGUS
          Where is Petrocom?

Monica is about to respond but she
realizes that she doesn't know and stops
short.

                    MONICA
          That is irrelevant.

Angus gets more worked up.

                    ANGUS
          Then why secure and hold
          for Petrocom if it is
          irrelevant?

These questions are making her brain hurt.
She recalls...

                    MONICA
          To make new worlds and new
          homes for mankind!

                    ANGUS
          Where are the mankinds?

Again, she's stumped. He turns his
attention to the computer files.

                    SHIP COMPUTER
          Accessing, GCS Comm. Last
          Communication.

He scrolls down to *Plant Shutdown*.

                    SHIP COMPUTER
          PLANT SHUTDOWN: All
          terraforming plants shut
          down according to UN
          regulation eight six three
          five six (No incomplete
          experiments shall be left
          unattended).

One of his screens has the list of Plants.

                    SHIP COMPUTER
          Accessing Plant 59: Ready.
          Plant 59 operation status,
          Inactive.
                    (pause)
          Accessing. Plant 59 is
          fully operational.

Angus and Monica stare at the screens.

                    SHIP COMPUTER
          Accessing. Listing all
          plants and their operational
          status: Plant 1: INACTIVE;
          Plant 2: INACTIVE; Plant 4:
          INACTIVE; Plant 5: INACTIVE;
          Plant 6: INACTIVE; Plant
          9: INACTIVE; Plant 28:
          INACTIVE--

Angus stops the list and speaks to the
computer.

                    ANGUS
          Are all plants inactive?

                    SHIP COMPUTER
          Yes.

Suddenly Monica looks at Angus.

                    ANGUS
          The plants are operational,
          but they are not operating.

She stares back at him.

                    MONICA
          Then, what is...the
          objective...of...all this?

Angus leans in as close as he can and
looks in her eyes.

                    ANGUS
          I...

Monica twitches as he says "I."

                    ANGUS
          ...don't know... We...are
          fighting...a cancelled
          operation.

She accesses the cover of the Annual
report.

                    ANGUS
          You...are fighting a
          cancelled operation--

                    MONICA
               (interrupting)
          Stop!

She holds up a hand. She's overloaded with
information. He stops and waits, watching
her eyes dart around, thinking.

Console screen: GeoConSolidated Annual
Report 2322. She looks at the screen.

                    MONICA
               (weakly)
          What is the current year?

Angus stares back at her, stumped. But
then he checks his clock on his data
screen.

                    SHIP COMPUTER
          Current year is four
          thousand, two hundred
          thirty one, solar time,
          also known as Earth time.
          The time is zero two--

                    MONICA
               (interrupting)
          What is year of crash of

                    transport?

                         SHIP COMPUTER
               Solar year, two thousand,
               three hundred twenty two.
               Lima year...

                         ANGUS
                      (whispered)
               One thousand nine hundred
               and nine years ago...

Monica and Angus stare at each other.

                         MONICA
               How long is that?

He looks at her and then shrugs through
his armor.

                         ANGUS
               I don't know...

They look at each other without
understanding what they've learned.

INT. OBSERVATION LOUNGE - DAY

Angus wakes up. Monica is nearby, sleeping.
They have their helmets on and are in an
upstairs section with large windows.

A storm outside batters the ship. Angus
watches as the atmosphere roils and
thunders. Periodically lightning cracks
down. The wind howls. It rocks the
wreckage. It's quite beautiful.

Angus looks at Monica. She's squatting,
asleep. He watches her quietly. He looks
out the windows again. The clouds are
changing. Suddenly a finger of atmosphere
starts to point down; a <u>funnel cloud</u>.

It forms swiftly, and powerfully. It pokes
the ground and sucks sand into the sky.

Now the HOWLING, battering wind is sandblasting the crashed ship. The funnel turns red the more sand it sucks up. It seductively curves and whips around.

Now it moves towards the ship.

Angus checks his data screens: WARNING! Cyclonic disturbance! Move to shelter!

Angus stands and moves over to Monica, touches her.

                    ANGUS
          Monica. Wake up. Monica!

She wakes.

                    MONICA
          Huh? Wha... What?

                    ANGUS
          A cyclonic disturbance.
          Stand up.

They scramble away from the windows. The funnel approaches the ship quickly. And then STRIKES the ship rocking it violently. The rocking becomes shaking and rattling.

The ship suffered severe damage in the attack and crash. This section does not have hull integrity. The buffeting shakes lose bulkheads and seals. The windows explode.

Loose objects get sucked out of the ship. Angus and Monica are pulled off their feet. The funnel sucks them towards the windows. They scramble to hold onto anything.

Sudden gusts pull them even harder outside. They push against the hull trying to stay inside.

And suddenly the hull rips open.

Angus and Monica get lifted into the funnel, SCREAMING.

[Angus flashes back to his memory, CRYING, the hand, his tear on his cheek.] TERROR.

Data screens are going crazy, flashing warnings at them to get their feet on the ground.

        ANGUS   MONICA
MONICA!   ANGUS!

EXT. PLANET SURFACE

The wind lifts them high in the air and carries them. It moves past the ship, destroying that portion.

These very heavy, Colonial Militants are twirled about like toys until they fall to the ground, scattered like the rest of the debris.

Monica has tucked into a ball and hits a dune like a meteor. She drives a groove into the sand and comes to rest.

Angus is buffeted by the wind and tries to curl up, but can't. He gets flung crashes into rocky terrain.

He rolls and tumbles and hits a few outcroppings, sending pieces flying. He settles, face down in the sand.

The storm crawls over them, giving them one or two final kicks, and gradually dies out.

They're breathing heavily. Angus has a strained expression on his face.

He contemplates what could have been his death. His expression tightens. He's definitely angry.

He tries to push himself up but falls. His
arm is damaged.

                    ANGUS
          Monica? Are you operational?
          Were you damaged?

                    MONICA
          Negative on damage...I——

The word "I" stops her, but she said it.

                    MONICA
          ...am operational.

He grunts and tries the other arm and gets
up to look around. He can't visually see
Monica anywhere nearby. They resort to the
data screens that show them on the map and
how far away they are from each other.

Angus stands fully, his damaged arm
hanging limp. His repair crabs emerge and
get to work.

She refers to her screens.

                    ANGUS (O.S.)
          Excellence. Recommend
          reconnoiter at azimuth
          forty-two dot seven tw——

Angus is looking at the blinking, a spot
in between them, on his heads-up display
(HUD). And then it CRACKS, continuing
from a dent in the helmet that frames the
faceplate.

ATMOSPHERE starts HISSING into his helmet.
He COUGHS, and SPLUTTERS.

                    MONICA (O.S.)
          Copy. Are you damaged?

He checks his diagnosis.

                    ANGUS
              HULL BREACH. FACEPLATE!

                    MONICA
               Can you plug it?

Angus' screens start to display his
predicament. Repair crabs come out and
immediately isolate the leak, but they need
to "REPLACE FACEPLATE." Monica sees that on
her data screens.

Angus is freaking out, trying not to
breathe. Flashes of ROACH dying hit him.
His huge hands are trying to block the
leak, but the crack spreads further,
diagonally across his faceplate.

                    MONICA
               Hit the ground! Dig in!

Angus looks around for help. He sees the
sand before him and dives head first into
it. His helmet creates an indentation. The
crabs struggle to keep working.

                    MONICA (O.S.)
               Use the sand to create a seal!

Monica is watching his POV on her data
screens. She turns and studies her area.
There's debris from the ship everywhere.
But the ship is now quite a way back.

Her screens show inventories and then
point her to a specific part of the
crashed transport GeoConSo Transport five
four three zero.

She starts running.

Angus burrows a deeper hole to fit his
whole faceplate and most of his helmet. The
crabs get the idea and help out, shoving
sand to block out the atmosphere.

Nonetheless, it's leaking in. Angus is tearing up and COUGHING. Ventilation in his helmet sucks out some of the atmosphere. Repair crabs inside his helmet try to plug up the leak by soldering the glass.

But Angus has to breathe that too.

EXT. CRASH SITE

Monica sprints to the transport. Minutes go by.

INT. GEOCONSO TRANSPORT FIVE FOUR THREE ZERO

She scrambles inside the payload area, looking.

                    MONICA
          How is the leak?

Monica can see her and Angus' data on her screens, but she asked anyway.

                    ANGUS (O.S.)
          Sustainable. The sand...is
          toxic.

EXT. PLANET SURFACE

Angus digs deeper into the sand.

INT. ANGUS' HELMET

Angus is breathing in spurts through his mouth, squinting his eyes against the atmosphere's effects. Hoses spray water mist on his eyes and face and suck it away.

                    MONICA (O.S.)
          Stay calm. I'll be there.

[CRYING Angus is freaking out. The blurry gloved hand reaches into his incubator and touches his cheek.]

                    ANGUS
          Affirmative.

INT. PAYLOAD BAY

Monica ransacks the area, her data screens
pointing her in various possible directions.
She opens a storage cabinet and finds
something!

EXT. PLANET SURFACE

Angus has submerged deeper in the sand.

INT. ANGUS' HELMET

The crabs stop working. They look around,
at a loss for what to do next. Angus is
not comforted by this.

EXT. PLANET SURFACE

Monica has emerged from the transport and
is running full speed, carrying a large
but apparently empty cargo case.

On her HUD she sees where Angus is supposed
to be, behind some rolling dunes, rock
formations and strewn debris.

Even though her suit is doing all of the
exertion, it still is a strain on her body.
Minutes go by as she closes the distance.

Finally, she clears a dune and finds Angus.

                    MONICA
          Here!

                    ANGUS (O.S.)
          Good!

She flips open the case, grabs a spare
helmet and places it next to Angus' head.

She shoves it into the sand about as deep as he is.

She takes the case, places it over his head and shoulders. The crabs consider the new situation and go back into action. More crabs come out of Monica's suit and join the project.

LATER

The crabs have made an enclosed workspace of the plastic case, cut it to fit Angus' neck to create a seal. They piled more sand over it to create the air pocket. Monica holds the case down to help keep the seal.

Inside they remove the broken faceplate, shove it aside just enough, and replace it with the spare.

LATER

The faceplate boots up and the last repair crabs finish sealing it in.

Angus blinks in relief. His face shows some irritation from his exposure, but crabs scurry about, treating his minor injuries. His eyes are red, but he's okay.

                    MONICA (O.S.)
          Are you operational?

Angus struggles to his knees, discarding the makeshift workspace. The crabs are working on his broken arm. He breathes deeply again.

                    ANGUS
          Yes...!

His expression seems to have an ANGRY determination.

                    MONICA
            What are we going to do?

                    ANGUS
            We're going to find Buddha.

EXT. DESERT PLAIN - DUSK

The world has taken a brilliant violet
glow as the sun sets. Gradually Angus and
Monica's helmet lights come on. They walk
together, reunited.

Angus has Eldon's tracks geometrically
projected onto his faceplate from a replay.

There are impressive mountains in the
distance, evidence of ancient oceans
carving this planet. The repair crabs
finish fixing his arm and return to their
homes, some return to Monica's armor.

They walk silently for a long time.

Angus is looking off into the distance,
almost mesmerized. Gradually, a POPPING
sound introduces itself. His eyes flicker
some wonder. He starts to notice the
POPPING sound.

He refers to his data screens. Nothing
abnormal. He looks up again. He looks
around, turns his head.

There's nothing in their immediate
surroundings that catches his attention. He
looks out further. Nothing in the expanse
ahead of them or the sky seems to be
producing the sound.

Angus is getting perplexed. He taps his
helmet.

                    ANGUS
            Monica?

                    MONICA
          Yes?

                    ANGUS
          Do you hear that sound? It...

They LISTEN. She looks around as Angus had
done. They look purplish as they trudge
along.

                    MONICA
          What sound?

                    ANGUS
          A...popping sound.

She listens. Closely.

                    MONICA
          No...Monica does not hear
          an anomalous sound.

Angus frowns, listens... Listens...

                    ANGUS
          It stopped... I can't hear it.

He frowns again. Gives up. They continue
walking. Minutes pass. As do meters.

POP.

He notices it again; Aha. The POPPING sound
coincides with their footsteps. Almost.
Angus stops walking.

Monica continues walking. Angus watches
her. The sound coincides with her
footsteps. She notices that Angus has
stopped. Monica stops walking. Turns
around.

                    MONICA
          What is it...?

                    ANGUS
          It stopped. Again.

Angus is confused.

                    ANGUS
          The sound. It started again.
          And now it stopped again.

They listen.

                    ANGUS
          It seemed to come from
          your footsteps.

                    MONICA
          Footsteps?

                    ANGUS
          Start walking again.

Unsure, but...she starts walking. Angus
listens carefully, watches her. She walks
around, purposefully.

                    MONICA
          Negative.

                    ANGUS
          Silence!

He listens some more. Monica walks some
more. Nothing. No popping sound. Angus is
frustrated.

                    ANGUS
          Ach...It's gone again.

She stops walking.

                    MONICA
          Have you run a helmet
          diagnostic?

                    ANGUS
          Yes. That's not it.

He grunts. Angus continues walking again.
Monica joins him. They continue quietly for

some time.

MUCH LATER

He's concentrating on the land ahead.
Eldon's footprints reappear in an area
untouched by the tornado. They look as if
drawn by a draftsman. They're slightly off
of the line projected by Angus' template.
Perfectly straight POP!

Angus hears it. POP!

He's getting upset. Frustrated. POP!

Furtively he looks around, searching for
that sound, like a hunter. He looks at
Monica's feet. The sound doesn't <u>always</u>
coincide with her steps.

He raises his eyesight from her feet up
her legs, her arms, her helmet. Her face.
Her mouth.

<u>Opening and closing her lips</u>. Unconsciously
she's making that POPPING sound with her
mouth. He maneuvers in front of her.

                    ANGUS
          It's you!

Mesmerized, she stops popping. Notices him.

                    MONICA
          What?

They stop walking.

                    ANGUS
          <u>You</u> are making that popping
          sound.

                    MONICA
          What?

                    ANGUS
          You've been making that

> popping sound. All this
> time. With your <u>mouth</u>.

                    MONICA
          Wha... Bu...

She looks lost. He replays video footage of
her face and her mouth. He transfers it to
her helmet.

She gapes at it. Nuances of expressions
flutter across her face. Embarrassment. The
corner of her mouth attempts a smile.

                    MONICA
          Sorry...I...

                    ANGUS
          Well...

He doesn't know what to do. His face also
fluctuates. He attempts to say something,
and then...

Starts GIGGLING.

She starts GIGGLING also.

It sounds insane, almost mechanical.
Unpracticed.

Now... She starts LAUGHING in earnest.

He does too.

They laugh more and more. It takes them
over. Each one making the other laugh
more. Uncontrollably. They laugh so much
and so hard that tears come to their eyes.

                    ANGUS
          ...It ...was ...you.

                    MONICA
          I...didn't...know.

The two of them stand in the middle of the

violet blue desert, laughing their heads off. Arms swinging carelessly. Stumbling around. Two huge Colonial Militants being...

SILLY.

On the horizon appear two brilliant slivers.

Slowly the twin planets rise. Almost full now. Intensely bright. It's almost like daylight. The planets are partially broken up by cirrus clouds. Angus and Monica's laughter has died down.

                    MONICA
                (astonished)
        ...Look!

They gaze at the sight. The planets' atmospheres create amazing colors. They're both astonished.

                    MONICA
        Have you ever seen anything
        like that?

Angus smiles before he answers. Frowns. He hesitates.

                    ANGUS
        Never...

He stops himself. He looks at Monica for help.

                    ANGUS
        Yes. Haven't you?

Monica thinks.

                    MONICA
        ...uh...yes. There is...some
        recollection.

They look at each other. Then back at the

sky.

They stare for a long while. Angus'
attention drifts from the planets to
another thought. Or other thoughts.

                    ANGUS
          Do you recall anything else?

That grabs her attention away from the
planets also. She looks at him, thinking
and nodding.

                    MONICA
          ...incomplete. A scrambled
          signal.

Angus nods.

                    MONICA
          Do you?

                    ANGUS
          Yes. Scrambled. I...remember
          seeing those planets like
          that. But not clearly...not
          until you indicated them.

Angus looks back at the sky.

                    ANGUS
          I remember many things...

(Baby Angus crying. Blurry shapes. A
rubber gloved hand, finger reaches down
and wipes away a tear.)

He sighs ruefully.

EXT. PLATEAU - DAY

Angus and Monica follow Eldon's tracks
across the plain. There are huge buttes on
the horizon.

                    ANGUS
          All of them seem the same.

                    MONICA
          Yes.

As they walk, the plain ahead of them
starts to look different. There are wisps
of black smoke trailing into the air. They
walk.

                    ANGUS
          It always ends the same way.

And walk.

                    MONICA
          Yes.

And walk.

                    ANGUS
          Have you ever secured a Tower?

And walk.

                    MONICA
          Uh...no. There is no recollection
          of ever securing a Tower.
                    (pause)
          ...ever.

                    ANGUS
          I don't either.

The plain in the distance attracts Monica's
attention.

                    MONICA
          We are approaching smoke.

He looks up.

                    ANGUS
          Copy.

As Angus and Monica approach the edge

of the plateau the valley below reveals itself. In the distance they see more smoke and...

A <u>particularly large tower complex.</u>

And a battle. Angus and Monica reach the edge. They see the Flying Vehicle picking off soldiers, scaling their numbers down to a non-threatening size.

It's been a very big battle. There are hundreds of soldiers lying on the ground, from both sides, injured and dying.

They can see the Tower's Defenders giving up the battle, letting the Flying Vehicle do it for them. The Defenders turn and go back to the Tower.

The Attackers, one by one, are neutralized. Left to repair themselves or become scrap for repair crabs.

Three, two, one. The Flying Vehicle drops the last Attacker.

Another battle is over.

Monica stares out at the battlefield. She glances at Angus. Angus is staring also. His mouth drops open. She notices.

> MONICA
>> What?

Angus doesn't respond.

> MONICA
>> Angus?

He blinks. Looks at her. She's nervous. He points at the Tower complex. Monica looks at the battlefield.

The Flying Vehicle circles the battlefield and then zooms over one of the hills

behind the Tower. Angus is scrutinizing
the valley floor

                    ANGUS
          There. See?

She looks.

                    ANGUS
          The OS17. The satellite link?

She looks at the Tower complex and sees
a dish antenna. It's on one of the higher
points of the complex. She looks back at
Angus.

                    MONICA
                 (whispered)
          Buddha?

He nods. They both nod at each other,
solemnly.

Angus and Monica descend from the plateau.
Loose rocks precede them. The littered
battlefield jumbles closer to them.

Dead soldiers are lying all around them.
Many were instantly destroyed. Others were
injured, some worse than others.

Now they're in REPAIR MODE.

Angus and Monica are now amongst them.
Repair crabs are starting to scurry all
over the place. HISSING from the crabs'
movements rises from the whole valley.

Angus is walking straight. Monica is
looking around at all the wreckage and
carnage. It all makes a great impression
on her. Angus walks directly to the Tower
complex walls. Monica trails behind a bit.

INT. TOWER COMPLEX

Angus goes to the doors. They're closed.
They stay closed even though he motions
towards them as if he were entering. He
steps back, surveys the complex. He turns
and goes to one end.

Monica lingers and then follows him.

                    MONICA
          This is the oxygenation
          section...

                    ANGUS
          Yes.

                    MONICA
          Where are you going?

                    ANGUS
          Recon.

She nods and joins him. They find a
building marked "B Wing." Angus and Monica
walk up to one of several large doors on
the side of the building.

They also remain closed. Angus goes over
to a panel on the side, opens it. Inside
is a lever; OPEN, CLOSE. He grabs and
pulls it down. The door opens.

They walk into the Receiving area from
Angus' dream.

INT. COMMAND CENTER

Computer screen: ACTIVITY IN B WING;
RECEIVING! Buddha has noticed.

INT. TOWER COMPLEX

It's a huge space, metal everywhere. A
flicker of recognition crosses Angus' face.

Ahead is the Assembly Room. He can see the armor building machines in the distance.

                    ANGUS
                  (whispered)
          ...I remember this place...

Monica barely hears him. He looks at her.

                    ANGUS
          Don't you?

She stops. She nods, slowly. He walks to the Assembly Room. Angus stares at the armor building machines, the platforms, all of the strange equipment.

He remembers. Everything is dormant right now. He climbs one of the platforms, walks around. Monica is also remembering. She's staring at everything, agape.

                    MONICA
          What is this?

                    ANGUS
          This is where...we were
          assembled.

Monica walks around. The Assembly Room is huge. There are multiple rows of machines. And each row stretches for a long distance to both sides.

Monica explores the back rows. Angus climbs down from the platform.

Monica finds more doors at one end of the Assembly Room. Angus joins her. She opens a door.

The door slides up: Dormitories. Angus and Monica step in. They walk onto a deck that stretches to either side like the Assembly Room.

On the other side of the deck is a row of
hundreds of elevators. Angus and Monica
stand between two elevators at a railing
and look out at a metal lattice of levels
about thirty feet from them.

Each level is covered with hundreds of
dormitories. Inside the capsules are <u>human
bodies</u>, sleeping.

Angus and Monica stare.

INT. COMMAND CENTER

Computer screen: LOCATE SOURCE OF
ANOMALOUS ACTIVITY!

INT. DORMITORIES

Angus and Monica continue to stare in
disbelief at the sheer volume of bodies
that must be stored here. There's a level
directly in front of them and lots of
levels above and below.

                    MONICA
          What is this...?

As they watch, one section of dormitories
comes to life. The capsules pop open.
Adolescent men and women stand up and
shuffle out in one direction.

                    ANGUS
          New soldiers.

Angus turns around and leaves the
dormitories. Monica turns too.

                    MONICA
          Where are you going?

                    ANGUS
          Looking for a terminal.

Monica follows him into the Assembly Room.

INT. ASSEMBLY ROOM

Angus finds a terminal near one of the assembly machines. He plugs in.

> MONICA
> Why?

> ANGUS
> See what is happening with those new soldiers.

A console screen turns on. A menu appears.

> COMPUTER
> Hi, Angus seven eight, seven three. May I help you?

This computer voice is similar to the ship computer. Angus makes an inquiry.

> COMPUTER
> What would you like to know about New Soldiers?

Angus makes another inquiry.

> COMPUTER
> I'm sorry. Cannot find directory. Access denied.

INT. COMMAND CENTER

Computer screen: ANOMALOUS ACTIVITY SOURCE LOCATED! Assembly Room: Console 7748.

INT. ASSEMBLY ROOM

Angus tries again.

> COMPUTER
> What would you like to know

about New Colonial Militia?

Angus makes another inquiry.

                    BUDDHA
          ANGUS 7873, what are you doing?

Angus freezes. Shocked. Frightened. He
catches his breath. Monica is also shocked.
Buddha's voice is completely different than
the computer voice. It doesn't bother to be
polite. It sounds impatient, busy.

                    MONICA
          Buddha.

                    BUDDHA
          ANGUS SEVEN EIGHT SEVEN
          THREE, what are you doing?
          RESPOND NOW!

Monica disconnects Angus from the
terminal. He snaps back with a gasp.

                    MONICA
          Move.

Angus gapes at her.

                    MONICA
          We have to go. Buddha
          knows you're here.

Angus nods. They run through the huge
Assembly Room and out.

EXT. VALLEY - BATTLEFIELD

Calvin is walking from the Tower to B
Wing.

He sees Angus and Monica run out the door.
They head through the battlefield back up
to the plateau. Calvin raises his laser
cannon and fires a warning shot.

Angus and Monica see it <u>pass</u>.

                    CALVIN (O.S.)
          Stop! Identify designation!

Angus shakes his head at Monica. She understands. They scramble around the injured soldiers and stop. They crouch down and hide from Calvin.

Calvin trudges onto the battlefield. He scans the bodies lying about. Angus and Monica are kneeling next to three or four soldiers in repair mode.

Calvin gets closer to them. He looks right at them but doesn't shoot. He can see them but can't see them. Angus slowly places a restraining hand on Monica's arm.

Angus turns off his suit, the lights and screens power down completely. Monica is surprised and looks at him quizzically. He nods emphatically to follow his example. She powers down her suit.

Calvin gets closer. He stops within ten feet from them and scans them. Repair crabs climb onto Angus and Monica; they're potential salvage.

Calvin's data screen shows him a layout of the soldiers around him. The <u>blank</u> slots are Angus and Monica as physical objects, just like rocks, terrain or dead soldiers. Calvin doesn't recognize them.

Angus' repair crabs come out and seem to have a discussion with the other nosy crabs. Some start taking apart Angus' repaired arm.

Calvin scans some more. He's looking <u>right at them</u>.

                    CALVIN
              Identify designation!

He can see Angus and Monica looking back
at him. More anxious than Angus, Monica
moves her head, eyes, and mouth, whereas
Angus remains still. But Calvin doesn't
seem to get it. He does a double, triple
take.

Some of the first rehabilitated soldiers
get up around the battlefield, drawing
Calvin's attention. He gives up, turns
around, and heads to the B Wing doors and
goes inside.

                    ANGUS
                  (muffled)
          That was Calvin.

                    MONICA
                  (muffled)
          What?

Angus powers up his suit. The foreign
crabs stop working abruptly now that the
suit is clearly operational. Angus' crabs
seem miffed and take parts back from the
nosy crabs and undo their "repairs."

Monica powers up too. Crabs scuttle off of
her.

                    ANGUS
          That was Calvin.

She can hear him clearly now over their
comms.

                    ANGUS
          Do you remember him?

Monica thinks about it. Shakes her head.

                    ANGUS
          We were with him. At the

last battle we fought.

She can't remember. He stands up and starts walking towards the slope.

                    ANGUS
          Let's go.

                    MONICA
          Where are we going?

                    ANGUS
          To watch from the plateau.

They weave around the bodies. Monica looks at all the soldiers, crabs busily at work. Her data screens identify all of the soldiers: STEVEN — rm; DOBEN — rm; SUZE — rm...

Monica slows down, looking at all of the soldiers.

                    MONICA
          Angus.

Monica stops walking.

                    MONICA
          Can you patch into these
          Repair Mode soldiers?

He stops walking and turns around to look at her. He looks at the soldiers, refers to his data screens in his helmet, looks back at her with an expression of interest.

                    ANGUS
          Yes...?

He kneels down to one of the soldiers. Checks him out.

                    ANGUS
          We can patch in and...

> MONICA
> ...neutralize their ENET-1
> microprocessors.

A genuine smile crosses his face as he nods more and more enthusiastically at her. After a moment it's infectious and she can't help but smile (a child's first accomplishment acknowledged...).

INT. ASSEMBLY ROOM

Calvin is walking around looking for Angus and Monica. He has his laser cannon out, swinging back and forth. He finds Terminal 77483 and plugs in.

INT. COMMAND CENTER

Computer screen: LOCATE ANGUS 7873, Last location: Assembly Room, Console 77483.

INT. ASSEMBLY ROOM

Calvin understands his latest orders better now and disengages to continue looking for them.

EXT. VALLEY - MONTAGE

Angus and Monica plug into several Repair Mode soldiers and when presented with the options to "Reset ENET-1" processors, they select <u>NO</u>.

END of MONTAGE

Angus and Monica scurry around from soldier to soldier disabling their ENET-1 microprocessors.

> MONICA
> Fourteen soldiers will be
> one hundred percent in ten

                    minutes, so far.

                         ANGUS
               Good.

INT. COMMAND CENTER

Buddha escalates its interest. Computer
screen: DEFENDERS ON ALERT; LOCATE
ANGUS 7873. Locate Colonial Militant not
transmitting recognition code.

EXT. B WING DOOR

It opens and Calvin comes out and heads
directly into the battlefield.

Calvin's data screen indicates the status
of the fallen soldiers as he's looking for
Angus.

EXT. TOWER

The doors open. The remaining Defenders
are standing at attention.

INT. COMMAND CENTER

Computer screen: DEFENDERS ACTIVE; LOCATE
ANGUS 7873. Locate Angus 7873. NEUTRALIZE!

EXT. VALLEY

The Defenders step outside. They raise
their laser cannons to firing positions.
Monica disconnects from a soldier, stands
up and notices the emerging Defenders.

                         MONICA
               Angus?

                         ANGUS
               What?

He looks up. She points.

                    MONICA
          Defenders.

He sees them.

                    MONICA
          But they can't see us.

                    ANGUS
          Yet.

He stands.

Calvin notices something on his data
screen.

                    CALVIN
          Angus seven eight seven
          three, Located.

Angus and Monica see Calvin's data screen
in their helmets as well and hear him.

                    CALVIN (O.S.)
          Vector seven two six...

                    ANGUS
          Keep working.

Monica hurries to another soldier as Angus
tries to evade Calvin. Calvin fires his
laser. It hits just in front of Angus.
Angus ducks, pivots and fires at Calvin.
Calvin ducks.

Angus runs for cover. The battlefield
has several craters from the various
explosions. Angus scrambles into a deep
crevasse.

Calvin has lost him momentarily. Monica
hurries to another soldier.

A laser blast hits two feet away from
Angus. He glances in its direction.

The Defenders see him.

There are about fifty of them. These are the Defenders that weren't injured and therefore didn't need repairing. They all start firing at Angus.

Angus hunkers down. The air around him SIZZLES from the crisscrossing beams.

Monica is frightened by the onslaught directed at Angus.

The Defenders flank Angus. They swing out to their left, and continue shooting at him.

Calvin is getting closer to him as well.

Angus crawls along looking for another hiding place. He reaches a point where he can see Calvin, aims and shoots, hitting his arm, knocking him down.

Angus climbs out of the hole and runs for another crater nearby. At the last moment a laser bolt hits him tossing him into the crater.

Before Monica disconnects from the soldier she's administering a menu appears on her data screen. She scrolls down to a specific item: ATTACK MODE!

She disconnects and runs to the side.

Angus is rolling over on his side surveying the damage he suffered. He's relatively okay. An armor plate is torn to shreds. The Defenders continue their fire.

Calvin is back on his feet and advancing. His data screens indicate the terrain and the crater Angus is hiding in. He's getting closer to him. Soon he'll be in range. He aims in preparation.

Angus looks over the rim of the crater.
Calvin is aiming at him. He ducks down. A
laserbolt hits Calvin.

Monica fires at him again. Another hit, but
it glances off as Calvin falls again.

She swings around and shoots at the
advancing Defenders. She hits several.
Their shooting is interrupted.

Monica's first shot went through Calvin's
shoulder. He struggles to make it work. He
stands again. He scans in her direction.
Spots her.

> CALVIN
> Second non-transmitting
> Attacker located. Vector
> four four seven...

Angus shoots at Calvin, making him duck.

Some Defenders turn looking for Monica. She
runs from her original location, trying to
evade their fire. Some spot her and start
shooting. She dives into a ditch and rolls.
She sits up and looks out.

The soldier she had adjusted sits up.
Instantly he turns around, locates the
Defenders and starts shooting. One of the
Defenders explodes-- a direct hit. Two
more go down.

Monica aims and launches a grenade
and another. They land in front of the
Defenders.

One of them steps right onto the first
as it EXPLODES taking his legs off and
flipping him backwards.

The second grenade goes off disabling
three more.

The other Defenders launch three grenades

at Monica. She scrambles out of the hole
and runs. She reaches another hole as
the first one BLOWS. Then the SECOND. And
THIRD.

The repaired soldier launches a grenade at
the Defenders. He runs to the side, away
from the return fire. The grenade EXPLODES.
Five Defenders; direct hit, destroyed.

INT. COMMAND CENTER

The Computer screen updates to: LAUNCH AIR
SUPPORT!

EXT. AUTOMATED HANGAR

Ceiling doors open on a part of this Tower
complex. The Flying Vehicle emerges from
its hangar.

EXT. VALLEY

The Flying Vehicle zips into the airspace
over the fighting. It slowly circles the
battlefield as if looking for a fugitive.

More injured soldiers start getting up,
having completed their repair routines. At
first they hesitate, studying the situation
but then they switch over to attack mode,
given the circumstances.

They stand up in different places.
Therefore they provide a confusing new
element for the Defenders to consider.

Four newly repaired soldiers are now
standing. They shoot their laser cannons
at the Defenders. The Defenders are taking
heavy casualties. The flying Vehicle
circles the battlefield again.

                    MONICA
          Angus. Report!

Angus turns to look for Monica. He's still
in the crater.

                    ANGUS
          Nominal. And you?

                    MONICA (O.S.)
          Nominal.

                    ANGUS
          The Flying Vehicle is active
          and engaged.

She spots it.

                    MONICA
          Copy.

Now there are a total of seven repaired
soldiers fighting the Defenders. They're
shooting everything they've got.

Five more Defenders drop. A Defender fires.
Hits a repaired soldier in the helmet,
blasting it apart. That soldier falls
backward.

Monica looks back at Angus. Calvin is
sweeping a stream of laser fire closer to
Angus.

                    MONICA
          ANGUS!

Angus launches a grenade at Calvin -
THUNK! It hits his laser cannon in the
trigger section.

The cannon misfires and explodes. Sparks
and smoke. The grenade is stuck.

Calvin looks at it, tries to shake it off.
He looks up at Angus.

Their eyes _meet_. Angus _grimaces_.

It EXPLODES, ripping Calvin's arm, side and head off.

The Flying Vehicle starts dropping laser bolts. Angus runs for another hole. A bolt misses him, barely. The repaired soldiers get hit. The beams cut three of them down.

Monica sees the Flying Vehicle resolving the battle quickly. She sees Angus run from one crater to another. The Flying Vehicle hovers above them. She fires at it.

It dodges and immediately fires back at her. The beam hits dirt. But the SHOCK-WAVE throws her back.

More repaired soldiers "wake" up to get hit by the enemy fire as soon as they go to Attack Mode.

A beam chases Angus to another crater.

Monica sits up. She sees the first repaired soldier shoot at the Flying Vehicle. He hits it on the side. The ship kind of shrugs it off and shoots back.

The soldier EXPLODES.

Monica sees his smoke drift up, the Tower standing behind it. And she sees...

The dish antenna.

She looks for Angus. Angus launches grenades, creating diversions. Then he runs for it.

BOOM. BOOM. BOOM, BOOM. BOOM.

Monica checks her cannon; Rockets! She's out of them. She grabs a nearby repairing soldier. Turns her over. Rockets! She loads it, with some panache, nonetheless, spinning the rocket.

Monica aims at the dish antenna.

Locks on target. Monica fires.

The Flying Vehicle pivots. It chases Angus again.

Monica's rocket snakes through the air right for the antenna.

TINK! It hits it straight on. The antenna SHATTERS.

The beams chase Angus. They cut through some soldiers on the ground. He runs to another crater. The beams catch up to him.

Angus stumbles. Rolls into a crater.

(Baby Angus crying! The tear on his face...)

The beams stop. The Flying Vehicle stops and hovers.

INT. FLYING VEHICLE

The Flying Vehicle's screen flickers. Reestablishes. The Flying Vehicle starts to circle the battlefield.

The Flying Vehicle's screen: Telemetry interruption. SWITCHING TO ONBOARD SYSTEM!

It's lost the Attacker/Defender designations and has to determine them on its own. It has to re-plot the battleground.

INT. COMMAND CENTER

Buddha is surprised: TELEMETRY INTERRUPTION -- TELEMETRY INTERRUPTION -- TELEMETRY INTERRUPTION

EXT. VALLEY

Angus looks up, around.

                    ANGUS
          MONICA? MONICA?

Monica looks at him.

                    MONICA
          Copy. Here.

                    ANGUS
          Excellence! Excellence! That
          was...great!

                    MONICA
          Yes, yes. Great. Roger. Great!

She looks around, grinning. The Defenders
are standing around, lost. More soldiers
are getting up after their repair routines.
They're lost too.

Angus scrambles out of the crater and
runs over to Monica. She climbs out of her
cover. He reaches her and impulsively hugs
her, metal CLANKING on metal. She doesn't
know what to do but smiles nonetheless.

They break and look around at the
battlefield. Monica has a big, unpracticed
smile on her face. She looks at Angus.

Angus is beaming. He holds up his thumbs.

                    ANGUS
          Excellence!

INT. FLYING VEHICLE

The Flying Vehicle's screen: RETURN TO
HANGAR/AWAITING ORDER!

EXT. VALLEY

The Flying Vehicle turns and leaves the battlefield.

INT. COMMAND CENTER

No one's listening to Buddha. Computer screen: RESEND COMMUNICATIONS -- RESEND COMMUNICATIONS...

EXT. VALLEY

Angus and Monica are amidst the confused, repaired soldiers wandering around. They're the only ones cheering.

Angus stops with an idea.

                    ANGUS
          Monica!

She looks at him and he's already hurrying into the Tower complex. She turns to follow.

INT. ASSEMBLY ROOM

Angus plugs into the terminal.

                    BUDDHA
          ANGUS seven eight seven
          three, what are you doing?

                    ANGUS
          Can you stop belligerent
          operations?

                    BUDDHA
          Yes.

                    ANGUS
          Have you received GCS
          Order eight six eight five

                  dot three three five?

Despite Buddha's pushy demeanor, it is a
computer and responds as one when queried.

                         BUDDHA
               Affirmative. GCS Order
               eight six eight five dot
               three three five, received
               and processed.

So, Buddha knows...Angus thinks for a long
while.

                         ANGUS
               Stop...all belligerent
               operations and tactics for
               all Colonial Militants on
               CEM.4 until further notice
               from GCS.

Angus looks at Monica, anxiously. Buddha
thinks and they wait nervously.

                         BUDDHA
               Belligerent operations
               discontinued until further
               notice.

Angus and Monica smile at each other.

LATER

Angus and Monica have been at this for a
while. Both are connected to the Terminal.
The computer screen on the terminal
indicates what Angus is accessing.

He selects and accesses "REFINERY."

Now their relationship with Buddha is
much like their relationship with the ship
computer on the downed transport. Angus or
Monica thinks and Buddha responds.

                         BUDDHA
               Powering up refinery.

They go down several checklists according
to the computer. They make sure that
the reactor is ready. Then they check if
there's raw material in the refinery.

Finally they turn on the Tower.

                    BUDDHA
          Powering up tower. Plant
          status: Active. Plant
          integrity: 100%. Refinery
          status: Active. Processing.

INT. REFINERY

Conveyor belts and sorters are moving tons
of soil through the processors. All of
the machinery points to the height of the
Tower.

That's where the END PRODUCT TURNS OUT.

EXT. TOWER COMPLEX

The battlefield has been cleared of
dead and injured soldiers. Rehabilitated
soldiers are walking around.

Repair crabs are working on the dish
antenna Monica shot. One of them, P-Vo,
looks up as the Flying Vehicle passes
overhead.

INT. FLYING VEHICLE

The Flying Vehicle's screen: ALL COLONIAL
MILITIA! HEAD TO PLANT #1.

EXT. TOWER COMPLEX

Angus and Monica emerge through the Tower
doors. The Flying Vehicle is far out
towards the horizon now.

The plain is peppered with thousands of soldiers returning from wandering the planet surface. They're all converging on this Tower complex.

Angus and Monica walk out to the center of the former battlefield. Some other soldiers also follow them out.

They stop and turn around. They look up at the Tower.

A huge puffy clean white plume is growing out of the top.

Angus and Monica look at each other and smile. They look up at the sky. The oxygenated vapor flows into the atmosphere.

It mixes with the clouds and creates a majestic turbulence.

A rainbow appears in the plume. Then a light rain starts to fall.

And a little patch of revealed sky slowly turns blue.

Angus turns to Monica, smiling.

                    ANGUS
          Look for the blue sky!

                                        FADE OUT
          THE END

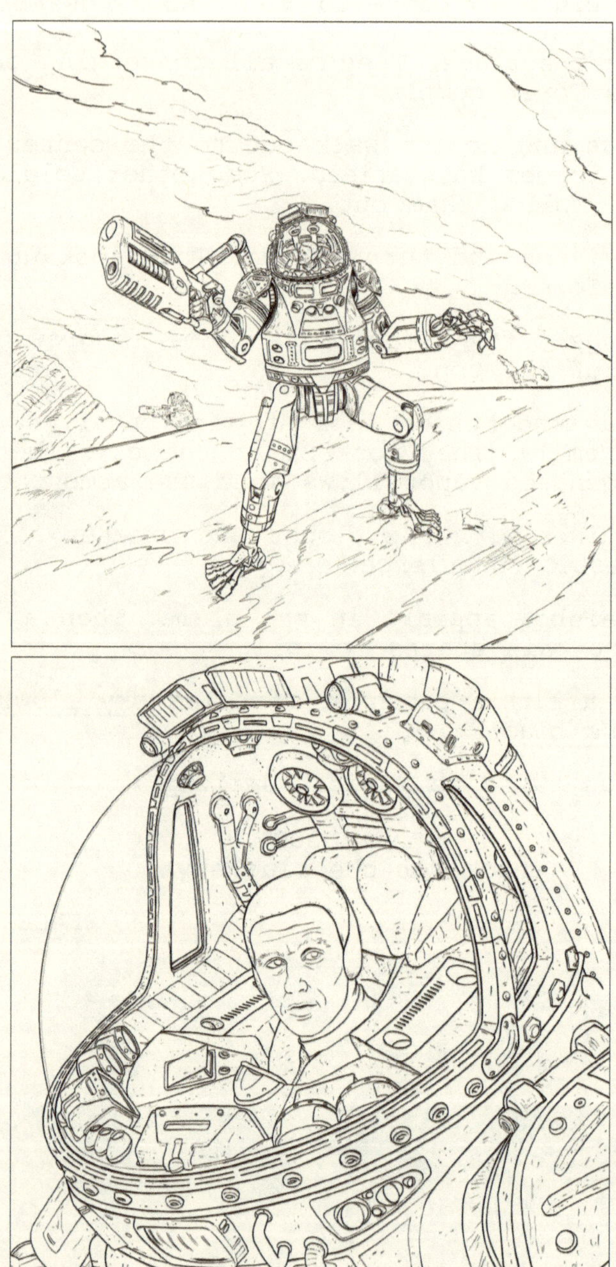

Oxygen Wars is being developed as a feature-length motion picture. It would consist of CGI effects and live-action actors.

If you'd like to support the project, please visit our Patreon page at: https://www.patreon.com/albinopiggorilla

To learn more about the movie project, please visit the AlbinoPigGorilla Studio website at: https://www.oxygenwars.com

www.ingramcontent.com/pod-product-compliance
Lightning Source LLC
Chambersburg PA
CBHW050455110726
47899CB00003B/952